"Cara. Not now. [...] here."

"But…" Her blue eyes were wide with bewilderment. "We're alone. We're married." And I want you. "Why not?"

He gave a little sigh, as much composed of regret as frustration at her lack of understanding. He glanced at his watch. "Because our departure has been arranged, right down to the last second. The car is timed to leave in half an hour—and after that, all the journalists will go away and file their copy. The guests cannot leave until we do—and I cannot leave prime ministers and presidents cooling their heels while I make love to my new wife!"

Millie flushed. "Of course not! How stupid of me!"

"Do not worry. You will learn." With the tips of his fingers, he tilted her face upwards. "There will be time enough for the pleasures of the bedroom…."

Sharon Kendrick

THE FUTURE KING'S BRIDE

THE
ROYAL HOUSE
OF
CACCIATORE

HARLEQUIN®

TORONTO • NEW YORK • LONDON
AMSTERDAM • PARIS • SYDNEY • HAMBURG
STOCKHOLM • ATHENS • TOKYO • MILAN • MADRID
PRAGUE • WARSAW • BUDAPEST • AUCKLAND

To Blackadder, with love.

ISBN 0-373-12478-3

THE FUTURE KING'S BRIDE

First North American Publication 2005.

Copyright © 2005 by Sharon Kendrick.

www.eHarlequin.com

Printed in U.S.A.

CHAPTER ONE

GIANFERRO had always chosen his mistresses well.

He looked for beauty and intelligence, but above all for discretion—for obvious reasons. Since the age of seventeen there had never been any shortage of willing candidates for this unofficial and unacknowledged place in his life, but that would have surprised no one. For even if you discounted the restless black eyes in the coldly handsome face, and his hard, lean body, there was not a woman alive who would not long to become a mistress to the Prince.

Especially a prince who would one day be King of Mardivino—the heavenly Mediterranean island over which his family had ruled since the thirteenth century. A prince who owned palaces and planes and fast cars, as well as a string of world-class racehorses. Untold wealth was at Gianferro's fingertips—and who could blame women if all they wished was for him to stroke those fingertips over their bodies?

But now his quest was different, and daunting—even for him. Before him lay possibly the most important decision he would ever make. He could put off the inevitable no longer. It was not a mistress he sought, but a bride.

And his choice must be the right choice.

His two brothers were now married and had produced children of their own—and therein lay the danger. There was one way and one way only to ensure that *his* bloodline inherited the crown of Mardivino.

He must marry.

His heart was heavy as he glanced around the bedroom he had been given when he'd arrived yesterday. It was very different from the architecture of his own Rainbow Palace, but it was still a very beautiful room indeed. He looked around him. Yes, a very English room.

The huge windows were composed of mullions and transoms and diamond panes which caught and reflected the light from many different angles, so that it resembled an interior as airy as a birdcage. But—his mouth twisted into an ironic smile—a cage from which he was unlikely to break free.

Caius Hall, an exquisite sixteenth-century house, was home to the de Vere sisters—the elder of whom he was intending to marry. Lady Lucinda de Vere—affectionately known as Lulu—was everything that he could want in a woman. Her blood was as pure as his, and she added blonde and beautiful into the bargain.

Their families had known each other for years—both fathers had studied together at university and had stayed in touch, though meetings had inevitably become fleeting and infrequent over time. Gianferro had even spent a holiday here once, but the two girls had been young then—indeed, one had been just a baby.

And then, late last year, he had met the older daughter at a polo match. It had not been by chance—but brokered by a mutual family friend who had thought it high time he meet someone 'suitable'. Almost without thinking, Gianferro had put his defences up, but he had been struck by Lulu's self-assurance and her outstanding beauty.

'I think I know you, don't I?' she had questioned cheekily as he bent to kiss her hand. 'Didn't you stay in my house once—years ago?'

'A long time ago.' He frowned. 'You were in pigtails and ribbons at the time, I believe,' he remembered.

'Oh. How very unflattering!'

But that long-ago meeting provided a certain kind of security, a bedrock which was vital to a man in his position. She was no stranger with hidden motives; he knew her background. The match would be approved by everyone concerned.

After that they had met several times—at parties which Gianferro knew had been laid on specifically for just that purpose. Sometimes he wondered: if he snapped his fingers and demanded the moon be brought to him on a plate, would a team of astronauts be dispatched from Mardivino to try and procure it for him?

Throughout their covertly watched conversations there had been an unspoken understanding of both their needs and wants. He wanted a wife who would provide him with an heir, and she wanted to be a princess. It was the dream of many an aristocratic English girl. As easy as that.

Today, after lunch, he was going to request that their courtship become formal. And if that invisible line was crossed there would be no going back. There would be subtle machinations behind the scenes in Mardivino and England as marriage plans were brokered, as he intended they would be.

In a few short hours he would no longer be free.

Gianferro allowed himself a brief, hard smile. No longer free? Since when had freedom ever been on the agenda of *his* life? Crown Princes could be blessed with looks and riches and power, but the liberties which most men took for granted could never be theirs.

He glanced at his watch. Lunch was not for another hour, and he was feeling restless. He had no desire to go downstairs and engage in the necessary small talk which was so much a part and parcel of his life as a prince.

He slipped out of the room and moved with silent stealth along one of the long, echoing corridors until at last he was outside, breathing in the glorious English spring air like a man who had been drowning.

The breeze was soft and scented, and yellow and cream daffodils waved their frilly crowns. The trees were daubed with the candy-floss pinks and whites of blossom, and beneath them were planted circles of bluebells, magically blue and, like the blossom, heartbreakingly brief in their flowering.

Taking the less obvious path, Gianferro moved away from the formal gardens, his long stride taking him towards the fields and hedgerows which formed part of the huge estate.

In the distance he could hear the muffled sound of a horse's hooves as it galloped towards him, and in that brief, yearning moment he wished himself astride his own mount—riding relentlessly along the empty Mardivinian shore until he had worn himself and his horse out.

He watched as a palomino horse streaked across the field, and his eyes narrowed in disbelief as he saw that the rider was about to make it jump the hedge.

He held his breath. Too high. Too fast. Too...

Instinct made him want to cry out for the horse to stop, but instinct also prevented him, for he knew that to startle it could be more dangerous still.

But then the rider urged the mount on, and it was one of those perfect moments that sometimes you witnessed in life, never to be recaptured. With a gravity-defying movement, the horse rose in a perfect, gleaming arc. For a split-second it seemed to hover in mid-air before clearing the obstacle with only a whisper to spare, and Gianferro slowly expelled the breath he had been holding, acknowledging with reluctant admiration the rider's bravery, and daring, and...

Stupidity!

Gianferro was himself talented enough a horseman to have considered taking it up as a career, had it not been for the accident of birth which had made him a prince, and he found himself tracing the deepened grooves of the hoof-marks towards the stables.

Perhaps he would advise the boy that there was a difference between courage and folly—and then perhaps afterwards he might ask him if he would like to ride out for him in Mardivino!

The scent of the stables was earthy, and he could hear nothing other than the snorts of a horse and the sound of a voice.

A woman's voice—soft and bell-like—as it murmured the kind of things that women always murmured to their horses.

'You darling thing! You clever thing!'

Gianferro froze.

Had a *woman* been riding the palomino?

With autocratic disregard, he strode into the tack-room and saw the slight but unmistakably feminine form of a girl—a *girl*!—feeding the horse a pepper-mint.

'Are you out of your mind?' he demanded.

Millie turned her head and her blood ran first hot, then cold, and then hot again.

She knew who he was, of course. Millie had often been accused of having her head in the clouds—but even *she* had realised that they had a prince staying with them. And that her sister Lulu was determined to marry him.

The place had been swarming with protection officers and armed guards, and she had heard her mother complaining mildly that the two girls who had been drafted in from the village to help had done very little in the way of work—the place was so filled with testosterone!

Millie had managed to get out of meeting the Prince at dinner last night, by pleading a headache—wanting to escape what she was sure would be a cringe-making occasion, while her sister paraded herself as though she was on a market stall and he the highest bidder—but now here he was, and this time there was no escaping him.

Yet he was not as she had thought he would be.

He did not look a bit like a prince, in his close-fitting trousers and a shirt which was undoubtedly silk, but casually unbuttoned at the neck to reveal a sprinkling of crisp dark hair. He was as strong and as muscular as any of the stableboys, with his hair as gleaming black as her riding boots. But blacker still were his eyes, and they were sparking out hot accusation at her.

'Did you hear me?' he grated. 'I asked whether you were crazy.'

'I heard you.'

Her voice was so low that he had to strain his ears to hear. He could see that she had been sweating—saw the way the thin shirt she wore clung to her small, high breasts—and unexpectedly a pulse leapt in his groin. There was no deference in her voice, either—didn't she know who he was?

'And are you? Crazy?'.

Millie shrugged. She had spent a lifetime being told

that she rode too fearlessly. 'That rather depends on your point of view, I suppose.'

He saw that her eyes were large and as blue as the flowers which circled the trees, and that her skin was the clearest he had ever seen—untouched by make-up and yet lit with the natural glow of exercise and youth. He found himself wondering what colour was the hair which lay beneath the constricting hat she wore, and now his heart began to pound in a way which made his head spin.

'You ride very well,' he acceded, and without thinking he took another step closer.

Millie only just stopped herself from shrinking away, but his proximity was making her feel almost light-headed. Dizzy. He was as strong as the grooms, yes, but he was something more, too—something she had never before encountered. When Lulu had spoken about 'her' Prince she had made him sound like nothing more than a title…she certainly hadn't mentioned that he had such a dangerous swagger about him, nor such an unashamedly masculine air, which was now making her heart crash against her ribcage. She stared into his dark eyes and tried to concentrate.

'Thank you.'

'Though whoever taught you to take risks like that should be shot,' he added darkly.

Millie blinked. 'I beg your pardon?'

'You'll kill yourself if you carry on like that,' he said flatly. 'That jump was sheer folly.'

'But I did it! And with room to spare!'

'And one day you might just not.'

'Oh, you can't live your life thinking like that!' said Millie airily. 'Wrapped up in cotton wool and worrying about what might happen. Timidity isn't living—it's existing.'

Something about her unaffectedness made him feel almost wistful. As did the sentiment. How long since he had allowed himself the luxury of thinking that way? 'That's because you're young,' he said, almost sadly.

'While you're a grand old man, I suppose!' she teased.

He laughed, and then stilled, the laughter dying on his lips, and something crept into the enclosed space of the stable—something intangible, which crackled in the air like the sound of the fresh, hot flames of a new fire bursting into life.

And as they stared at each other, another debilitating wave of weakness passed over her. Millie was brave and fearless on horseback, but now she prickled with a feeling very like fear, and the sweat cooled on her skin, making her clammy and shivery. As if she had suddenly caught a fever.

'I'd better finish up here,' she said awkwardly.

'Who are you?' he questioned suddenly. 'One of the grooms?'

Some self-protective instinct made her unsure what to say. If he thought she was just one of the hands he would be out of here like a shot. And I will be safe, she thought. Safe from that dark, dangerous look and that unashamedly sexual aura which seemed to shimmer off his olive skin.

'Yes,' she said. 'I am.'

For a moment a cold, hard gleam entered his eyes—a sense of the condemned man being offered one final meal before his fate was sealed. Her lips were curved, slightly open, and he could see the moist pinkness of her mouth. He longed to kiss her as he had never kissed a woman before, nor ever would again.

And Millie saw it all played out in that one, lingering look. She was almost completely innocent of men, but she had observed enough of nature to know what passed between the sexes. She knew exactly what was going on in the mind of the Prince, and for a moment her heart went out to her sister. What if he turned out to be the kind of man who played away? Serially unfaithful—just as their own father had been?

But Lulu would handle it; she always did. She had had men eating out of her hand for years, and why should this man be any different? But this man *was* different—and not just because he was a prince. He was...

Millie swallowed.

He was fantasy come true—virile and strong and masculine—even she could sense that. And women would always gravitate towards him, in the way that a mare always went for the most robust of the stallions. Her feelings did a rapid turnaround, and for a moment Millie almost envied her sister.

She stared for a second at the arrogant thrust of his hips and found herself blushing—terrified that he might be able to guess what she had been thinking. 'I...I'd better go,' she stammered.

He laughed again, but this time the laugh was regretful, and tinged with something else which he couldn't identify. 'Yes, run along, little girl,' he said softly.

'But I'm nineteen!' she defended, stung.

'Better run along anyway,' came the silky response.

She stared into the dark glitter of his eyes and did exactly what he said—rushing from the stable as if he was chasing her, out into the spring day which had been transformed by the mercurial April weather. Where before there had been bright sunshine now the clouds had suddenly split open, and rain was cascading down. But at least the droplets cooled her hectic colour and flushed cheeks as she dazedly made her way back to the Hall.

Wet through, she leaned against the wall of the kitchen-garden as she steadied her breathing. But her mouth felt as dry as summer dust, and her heart was still pounding as if it wanted to burst out of her chest.

She felt as if she was a cauldron, and he had reached inside and stirred up all her feelings, so that she was left feeling not like Millie at all, but some trembling stranger to herself.

And she still had lunch to get through.

CHAPTER TWO

'MILLIE, you're late!'

Above the hubbub of chatter, Millie heard the irritation in her mother's voice. It was a voice which had been trained to rarely express emotion, but under circumstances such as these, with one daughter poised to marry into such an exalted family, it was easy to see her customary composure vanish when the other turned up unacceptably late.

Millie had tried to slip unnoticed into the Blue Room, where everyone had gathered before lunch, but the majority of the guests were thronged around the tall, imposing figure of the Prince. 'Sorry,' she said, her eyes looking down at the priceless Persian carpet because she did not dare to look anywhere else, terrified to look into those dangerous, dark eyes...because...

Because what? Because in the time it had taken her to wash the mud and grime and sweat from her body and to dress in something halfway suitable she had been able to think of nothing other than the shockingly handsome man who would one day become her brother-in-law? Trying not to imagine what it would have been like if he *had* kissed her.

'Millie, it's just not *done* to keep Royalty waiting,'

16

scolded her mother, and then added in an aside, 'And couldn't you have worn some lipstick or something, darling? You can look so pretty if you put your mind to it!'

The implication being that she didn't look at all pretty at the moment. Well, that was a good thing. She wanted to fade away into the background. She didn't want him looking at her that way. Making her feel those things. Making her ache. Making her wonder…

'But I'd have been even later if I'd stopped to do that,' Millie protested, and then a dark shadow fell over her, and she didn't need to look up into that hard and handsome face to know whose shadow it was. She found herself having to suppress a shiver of excitement as he came to stand beside them and hoped that her mother hadn't noticed.

'Prince Gianferro,' said Countess de Vere, with the biggest smile Millie had ever seen her give, 'I'd like you to meet my younger daughter, Millicent.'

Millie risked glancing up then—it would have been sheer rudeness to do otherwise—and she found herself staring up into his face, all aristocratic cheekbones and dark, mocking eyes. *Say you've met me,* she silently beseeched him. Say that and everything will be okay.

But he didn't. Just lifted the tips of her fingers to his lips and made the slightest pressure with his mouth, and Millie felt a whisper of longing trickle its way down her spine.

'*Contentissimo,*' he murmured. 'Millicent.'

'Millie,' she corrected immediately as she dragged her hand away from the temptation of his touch and met his eyes in silent rebuke, some of her fearlessness returning to rescue her. 'Should I curtsey?'

His mouth curved. 'Do you want to?'

Was she imagining things, or was that a loaded question and—oh, heavens—why was she even *thinking* this way? He was Lulu's, not hers—and by no stretch of the imagination could he ever be hers—even if Lulu *wasn't* in the picture.

She nodded her head as she dipped into a graceful and effortless bob, hoping that the formal greeting would put proper distance between them.

'*Perfetto,*' he murmured.

'Yes, it was an *excellent* curtsey, darling,' said her mother, with a glow of slightly bemused satisfaction. 'Now, please apologise to the Prince for your lateness!'

'I—'

His eyes were full of devilment. 'I expect you had something far more exciting to do?'

He was weaving her deeper into the deception, and she was wondering how he would react if she said something like, *You know perfectly well what I was doing*, when to her relief the lunch bell rang.

'Lunch,' she murmured politely.

'Saved by the bell,' came his mocking retort, and Millie saw her mother blink, looking even more bemused.

Probably wondering how her mouse of a daughter had managed to engage the Prince's interest for more than a nanosecond!

There were twenty for lunch, and—as Millie had fully expected—she was seated at the very end of the table, about as far away from him as it was possible to be. And I hope you're enjoying your lunch, she thought, because every mouthful I take is threatening to choke me!

But Gianferro was not enjoying his lunch, and course after course made an appearance. The food was sublime, the surroundings exquisite and the company exactly as it should be—except…

His eyes kept straying to the girl at the end of the table. How unlike her sister she was. Lulu was as pampered and as immaculate as a world-class model—while Millie wore a simple dress which emphasised her long-limbed and naturally slim body. Her pale blonde hair was tied back and her face was completely free of make-up, and yet she looked as fresh and as natural as a bunch of flowers.

From close at his side Lulu leaned over, and he caught a drift of her expensive French perfume. Inexplicably he found himself comparing it to the earthy scent of horses and saddlesoap.

'You haven't touched your wine, Gianferro!' Lulu scolded.

He shrugged. 'Did you not know that I never drink at lunchtime?'

'No, I didn't! How boring!' Lulu pulled a face. 'Why ever not?'

'I need to have a clear head.'

'Not always, surely? Isn't it nice sometimes to be… um…' She shot him a coquettish glance. '*Relaxed* in the afternoon?'

He knew exactly what she was suggesting, and found himself…*outraged*. Or maybe, he admitted with painful honesty, maybe he was just looking for an excuse to be outraged. But it was more than that. Gianferro was an expert where women were concerned, and today he had seen Lulu on her home territory—and instinct told him that she was not what he wanted.

She was beautiful, yes—and confident and alluring—but her manner had been predatory since he had first set foot in her house, and while it was a quality which was admirable in a mistress it was not what he wanted from a wife.

Now she was flicking her hair back and letting her fingertips play with her necklace—all signs of sexual attraction, which was well and good. But he had realised something else, and he knew deep down that his instinct was the right one.

She was not a virgin!

Whereas Millie…

His gaze flicked down the table and he found her eyes on him. Huge and blue, confused and troubled. And as their eyes met she bit her lip and turned away, as if she had been stung.

Once again he felt the unexpected throb of a desire so primitive that it felt like something deeper than desire.

'Gianferro?'

He gave his most bland and diplomatic smile as he turned to the woman by his side. *'Sì?'*

Lulu's eyes were shining with undisguised invitation. 'Would you like me to show you round the estate this afternoon? I mean, *properly*?' She smiled. 'There are all kinds of hidden treasures in Caius Hall.'

Gianferro steeled himself. All his life he had controlled—had chosen the correct path to take—and yet the route he had been following had suddenly become blurred. He knew that the unspoken understanding which had existed so precariously between himself and Lulu would now never be voiced. No offer had been made and therefore there could be no rejection.

She would know, of course, and be disappointed—yes, invariably—but far better a mild disappointment at this early stage than engaging in something which he knew would never work.

He knew what he should do. Walk away today without looking back—but now he found he had chanced upon an unexpectedly clear path to take. His route no longer seemed blurred at all.

'Shall we all move places for dessert?' questioned Millie's mother.

Gianferro nodded. 'Indeed. I should like the chance to talk to both your daughters.'

It was undeniably a command, and the very last

thing she wanted—*or was it?*—but Millie knew where her duty lay, and she took her place next to him with a fixed smile on her face, trying to ignore Lulu's mutinous expression and wondering what on earth she was going to say to him.

Or he to her!

His smile was mocking as he bent his head to talk in a low voice. 'So why did you lie to me, Millie? Why did you pretend to be one of the grooms?' he accused softly.

Millie bit her lip. There was no way she could come out and explain that he had made her feel all churned-up and confused. He would think she was *mad*!

'Just an impulse thing,' she said truthfully.

He raised his dark brows. 'And are you often given to impulse?' he queried.

'Sometimes,' she admitted. 'Are you?'

He gave the same kind of almost-wistful smile he had shown her earlier and shook his head. 'Alas, such an indulgence does not go with the job description.'

'Of Prince?' she teased.

'Crown Prince,' he teased back.

'But you're a person as well as a title!' she declared.

How beautifully passionate she was, he thought. And how hopelessly naïve. 'The two are inextricably linked,' he said softly.

'Oh.'

'Anyway,' he said firmly, 'it is boring to talk of such things. Tell me about you, Millie.'

'Me?' She blinked in astonishment.

'Is that such a surprising thing to want to know about?'

She didn't want to say yes. To tell him that when you had an especially beautiful older sister very few people were interested in *her*. But he began to ask her about her childhood, and seemed genuinely to want to hear about it, and Millie began to relax, to open up. That strange and rather fraught encounter of earlier melted away as she began to tell him about the strictures of her life at the all-girls boarding school she had attended and about the jokes they had played on the nuns. And when his dark eyes narrowed and he began to laugh Millie felt as though she had achieved something rather special.

Until she realised that the whole table had grown silent, and that everyone was looking at them—her mother in surprise and Lulu with undisguised irritation.

'What would you like to do this afternoon, Gianferro?' questioned her mother.

He saw Lulu raise her eyebrows at him.

'I will tell you what I would like to do,' he said softly. 'I should like to go and look at your horses.'

Lulu grimaced. 'The *horses*?'

'But, yes,' he murmured. 'I have many fine mounts in Mardivino, and I should like to see if you have anything here to equal them.'

'Oh, I think you'll find that we do!' laughed one of the men.

From the centre of the table Lulu waved a perfectly manicured hand, first towards the window and then against her shell-pink couture gown. 'But it's *raining*!'

'I like the rain,' he said softly.

Lulu tapped her fingernail against the polished wood. 'Well, if you want to get soaking wet, that's fine by me—but don't expect me to join you!'

There was an infinitesimal silence. He could read in her eyes that she now fully expected him to capitulate, to say that he had changed his mind and would see the horses another time, but he would never do that. Never. Never would he bend his will to a woman!

'As you wish,' he said crisply.

His displeasure was almost tangible, and Millie saw her mother's stricken face as her lunch party threatened to deteriorate. She licked her lips nervously. 'I could show the Prince the horses, if you like?'

Her mother gave her a grateful smile, which only added to Millie's growing sense of discomfort. And guilt. 'Oh, darling—*would* you?'

Gianferro smiled. 'How very kind of you, Millie. Thank you.'

The easy atmosphere had evaporated and now the tension was back. Her heart beating hard against her ribs, Millie pushed her chair back, hating him for the way he was behaving and hating herself just as much, without quite knowing why.

'Come on, then,' she said ungraciously, and was rewarded with a slight narrowing of his eyes.

'But you'll need to change!' objected her mother.

'Oh, I'm okay—a little bit of rain never hurt anyone,' said Millie firmly.

Lulu gave an edgy laugh. 'Millie won't care if she gets soaked to the skin—she's such a *tomboy*!'

It was the kind of taunt which had haunted her down the years, but Millie didn't feel a bit like a tomboy as Gianferro followed her and the room fell silent. Inexplicably—and uncomfortably—she had never felt more of a woman in her life.

At the east entrance, she opened the door. Beyond the rain was an almost solid sheet of grey.

She turned to him. 'You can't honestly want to go out in that?'

'Yes. I do.'

She grabbed a waterproof from the hook and half threw it at him before pulling on one herself. 'Come on, then.'

Perversely, he liked the ungracious gesture, and the angry look she sparked at him as he pulled on the battered old coat, with its smell of horses and leather. He stepped outside and felt the rain in his hair and on his cheeks. It was coming down so fast that when he opened his mouth it rushed in—knocking all the breath out of him.

'We'll have to run!' said Millie, but suddenly she

felt a strange sense of excitement. The dull, formal lunch had become something else. He wanted to see her beloved horses, and this was where she felt at home. *But it is more than just that, Millie, and you know it is.* She shook her head, as if she could shake away the troublesome thoughts. 'Come on!'

Laughing with a sudden recklessness which was alien to him, he ran behind her, dodging puddles and watching as the mud splattered droplets up her pale silk-covered legs. Tights? he wondered. Probably. She was too gauche and unworldly to pull on a pair of stockings. What was he doing here, and why was he allowing this to happen? This was craziness. Madness. He should stop it right now.

Yet all the time a feeling was growing deep inside him, a sense of the irrevocable about to happen, as though his fate was about to be sealed in a way in which he had least expected.

By the time they reached the stables Millie's hair was plastered to her skull, and she turned to him, brushing cold droplets of rain away from her skin as if they were tears, not knowing and not caring what was the right thing to say any more.

'Why didn't you tell my mother we'd already met today?'

'You know why.'

'No, I don't.'

'Yes, you do. Just as you know what is going to happen next.'

She shook her head, trying to quell the glow of

excitement, trying to pretend it wasn't happening. 'You're talking in riddles!'

'Why did you agree to bring me here, Millie?' he questioned silkily.

'Because you...because you wanted to look at the horses, didn't you?'

In any other woman it would have been a coy question, but Gianferro knew she meant it. 'No. You know very well what I wanted. What I want. What you want, too—if you can dare to admit it to yourself.'

Her eyes were like saucers as she saw the expression on his face and read the sensual intent there, so dark and so powerfully irresistible that she shook her head, willing it to go away even while she prayed it never would. 'No,' she breathed. 'No. We mustn't!'

'But we have to—you know we do,' he whispered. 'For you will die unless we do.' And so will I.

'Gianferro!'

He pulled her into his arms and tumbled her down beneath him onto the spiky bed of a bale of hay, pushing back a strand of hair from her rain-wet face. For one long moment he stared down at her, ignoring the bewilderment in her eyes, before blotting out the world with the heady pressure of his kiss.

For Millie it was like jumping the highest jump in the world—she'd never felt such a heady blend of excitement and fear before. She could feel the muscular strength of his body, and his hands cupping her face, his lips grazing over hers.

'Oh!' It was a broken plea, a request for something

she wasn't aware she wanted, and as she made it he opened her lips with the seeking brush of his tongue. She gasped as it flicked inside her mouth. Fireworks exploded inside her head and she began to ache as she gripped onto him, drowning in the sweetness of it all, her body seeming to take on a life of its own as it pushed itself against the hard sinews of his. Dimly, she was aware of the heavy flowering of her breasts, and their sweet, prickling ache made her want him closer still.

With a terse exclamation he pulled himself away from her, his breathing ragged and unsteady as he stared into the sultry protest of her slick lips.

'Why did you stop?' she questioned, in a honeyed voice which sounded like a stranger's.

'Why?' He gave a short laugh. 'Why do you think?' And then he read the uncertainty and the hunger in her big blue eyes and relented, his dark brows knitting together. 'Have you ever kissed a man before, Millie?'

She stared at him. So he had guessed! 'Not…not like that.'

The dark brows were elevated in lazy question. 'And what way is that?'

She wanted to say *With your tongue*, but she couldn't. It made it sound so anatomical. As if what had just happened had been all about experimentation, and it had not been about that at all—more a great whooshing feeling which had swept her away and made her feel like…like…

She shook her head, as if that could make the mixed-up feelings go away. 'Nothing.'

A sense of triumph began to bubble up inside him as he acknowledged just how inexperienced she was, and he pulled her back into his arms. 'You kiss very beautifully,' he said softly. 'Very hard and very passionately.' He traced the outline of her lips with the tip of his finger and they trembled beneath his touch. 'But there are other ways to kiss a man too, and I shall show you them all. I shall teach you well, dear Millie.'

His words seemed to bring her to her senses, and she pulled herself away from him. He did not stop her. What the hell was he suggesting? What had he lured her into, and why had she *let* him? Distractedly, she tugged strands of hay from her hair and cast them down on the stable floor as she stared at him.

'You won't do anything of the sort!' she spat out, her voice shaking with emotion. 'What kind of man do you think you are?' *And what kind of woman was she?* 'You're going to marry my sister!'

He shook his head. 'No,' he said heavily. 'I am not.'

'You are! You are!' she cried desperately. 'You know you are!'

'I cannot marry her,' he said flatly, and he reached out and captured her chin, turning her face towards his to imprison her in the ebony spotlight of his gaze, melting her with its intensity. 'And we both know why that is.'

CHAPTER THREE

'I'M GOING to marry Gianferro.'

Lulu paused in the act of brushing her hair. 'Are you out of your tiny?'

Millie swallowed, but the words had to be said, no matter what the reaction. 'I'm sorry.'

The eyes which were reflected in the dressing-table mirror narrowed, and then Lulu whirled round. 'What the hell are you talking about?'

'Gianferro, and I...we are to be married.'

'Tell me you're joking.'

Millie shook her head. The right thing to say now would be, *I wish I was,* but that wouldn't have been true. And she had decided that she could not shirk the truth. Lulu was going to be hurt—through no fault of her own—and it was Millie's duty to stand there and take the flak. 'No. I'm not joking.'

For a second Lulu's mouth twisted, and then she said, in the same voice she used to use when she told Millie that men didn't like girls who smelt faintly of manure, 'Millie—you may have decided to develop a crush on that cold-hearted bastard, but it really isn't a good idea to start living in fantasy land. If you come out with bizarre statements like that then people are bound to get to hear. And people will laugh.'

'She means it, Lulu,' said a voice at the door, and both sisters turned round to see their mother standing there.

'You knew?' questioned Millie in bewilderment.

'Gianferro rang me this morning,' said her mother. 'Supposedly to ask my permission for your hand, since your father is no longer with us—though I got the distinct impression that my agreement was academic. That he intends to marry you whether I sanction it or not, and that he is not the type of man who will take no for an answer.'

Lulu was looking from one to the other, like a spectator at a tennis match, a look of puzzlement on her face. 'But she doesn't even *know* him!'

There was an uncomfortable silence.

'How can she be marrying him?' continued Lulu, in disbelief. 'If she hasn't seen him since that day he ruined our lunch party and broke my heart into the bargain?'

'He didn't break your heart, darling,' said her mother gently. 'You've been back with Ned Vaughn ever since!'

But Lulu wasn't listening. 'Are you going to give us some kind of explanation, Millie? You've only met him once!'

The Countess's eyes were shrewd. 'I think you'll find she's met him a great deal more than once—haven't you, Millie?'

Millie nodded, biting her lip, summoning up more courage than she had ever needed in her life.

'When?' snapped Lulu. 'And where?'

'At Chichester. And Cirencester. Once in Heathcote.'

Lulu's eyes narrowed. 'At *horse* fairs?'

'That's right. Well, where the horse fairs were being held. We didn't actually go to any.'

There was silence for a moment, and then Millie drew a deep breath as she met the question in her sister's eyes. Just tell it. Tell it the way it is—because that way you might be able to believe it yourself.

'He wanted to see me again and thought we should meet up at places that I actually had a legitimate reason to visit—that it would be the best way to avoid suspicion.'

'Why, you sneaky little cow!'

'Lulu!' said their mother warningly.

'No,' said Millie. 'She has every right to say it. And more.' Her voice was even lower than usual. 'I'm truly sorry, Lulu—I really am. I didn't mean for it to happen, and neither did he. It just did.'

Lulu gave a high, forced laugh. 'You little fool!' she spat. 'Don't you know he's just been spinning you a line to get you into bed? Your first lover! Don't you realise that for a man who has everything—and has *had* everything—a woman's virginity is something you can't put a price on?'

'We haven't...' Millie's words tailed off as she registered the incredulous look on Lulu's face. 'Nothing has happened between us, and nothing will—at least not until after the wedding. That's the way Gianferro wants it.'

'"*That's the way Gianferro wants it!*"' mimicked Lulu furiously.

'I wanted you to be the first to know, Lulu—'

'Well, thanks! Thanks for nothing!' Lulu's eyes narrowed again, and this time her rage reminded Millie of the time when she had been turned down for the starring role in the school pantomime. 'You must have told him!'

'Told him what?'

'That I'd been...' Her breathing quickened. 'Did you blab about me and Ned? Did you tell him that we'd been lovers?'

'Of course I didn't!' Millie cried, appalled.

'There's no "of course" about it! You were obviously determined to get your hooks into him, and it seems you've succeeded! Or are you really expecting me to believe that he came here with *me* in mind and changed his mind when he saw *you*?'

'I don't know how or why it happened,' said Millie miserably. 'It just did.'

'Well, may I offer you my congratulations, darling?' came a gentle voice, and Millie jerked her head up, looking at her mother with tear-filled eyes. 'We must be glad for your sister, Lulu,' she added firmly.

'You just want one of your daughters to marry into Royalty!' said Lulu crossly. 'You don't care which one!'

'Nonsense! You'll be perfectly happy as a wealthy

landowner's wife, ordering Ned here, there and everywhere—you know you will. Gianferro would never have suited *you*, my darling—you're much too independent of spirit.'

Lulu looked slightly mollified, but she wasn't finished with her sister yet. 'And do you really think—with your zero experience of men—that you can handle a man like Gianferro?'

Millie stared at her. 'I don't know,' she said honestly. 'All I know is that I've got to try.'

The Countess pushed her gently down onto a chair. 'Won't you tell us how it happened, darling?'

Millie knew that she owed her family some kind of explanation—but where to begin? And how much would Gianferro be happy for her to reveal?

Already she was aware of the great gulf between her and the rest of the world—one which was widening by the second. She was to be the future King's bride, and with that came responsibility—and distance. Gianferro was not a man like other men—she could not gossip about what he'd said to her. There could be no blushing disclosures of how he had asked her to marry him. But there again, thought Millie, with a touch of regret, it was not the kind of proposal which would go down in history as one of the most romantic. No, for Gianferro it was a purely practical arrangement. She understood that was the way it had to be.

There had been a series of meetings—carefully arranged and discreetly choreographed. Silent, purring cars had been dispatched to collect her from train stations, whisking her away to various houses—safe houses, she believed they were called—where Gianferro would be waiting for her. The armed guards and the protection officers had been kept very much in the background—like crumbs swept away before the guests arrived.

Their hosts had often been strangers to her, but she had known one of the couples fairly well. She remembered the hostess looking her up and down, unable to hide her expression of faint surprise. Yet Millie knew that those meetings would not be spoken of. Not even to her mother—not to anyone—because Gianferro would have demanded total confidentiality and because the stakes were too high. *What stakes?* she asked herself, but it was a question she did not dare answer, just in case she was hopelessly off the mark.

There had been small lunch parties, when she'd been gently quizzed on her attitude to politics and art—what she thought of the women's movement. Her responses had come over as quite lukewarm—even to her own ears—and it had made Millie realise how insular her life was, how little she really thought about—other than her horses.

I am being tested, she'd thought suddenly. *But for what?*

Yet she had known, deep down, just what was expected of her—and exactly how to behave—for in a way hadn't she been brought up to do exactly this?

One day she'd been chattering her way through a tour of some magnificent gardens—properly showing interest in all the trees and shrubs. She'd seen their host nodding, and Gianferro's look of satisfaction as she recognised the bud of a rare Persian rose. She'd felt as if she was jumping through hoops.

Afterwards, it should have been a treat to be shown the magnificent Andalusian horses which were stabled there, but for the first time in her life she had found she wanted to be elsewhere, not here—no matter how magnificent the breed. Alone with the tall, brooding man who was still such a stranger to her. The man who had occupied every second of her waking hours—and the dreaming ones, too—ever since he had blazed into her life with all the force of some dark and dazzling meteor. She had shot him a glance, but his intention had been focused firmly on the horses.

His manner was so formal towards her—there had been no repeat of that wild intimacy which had taken place in the stables that rainy afternoon. She found herself aching for him to take her into his arms again, but the longer it became, the more impossible seemed the very idea that the whole thing had ever happened. As if she had merely imagined it. Her increased exposure to him had only served to emphasise how gorgeous he was—yet he seemed more remote, and Millie's confusion grew at the same rate as her longing for him.

She had smoothed her hand over the gleaming roan

flesh of a horse. 'She's beautiful, isn't she?' she questioned tentatively.

'Not bad,' he murmured.

'Not bad?' laughed their host. 'This is the horse of Kings—and this particular mare will breed you future champions! She is yours, Gianferro!'

'You are too generous!' he protested.

'Yours,' emphasised the host softly.

'Thank you.' Gianferro inclined his head, acknowledging the honour, but knowing that no gift came without expectation. It had happened all his life, but now it was with increasing regularity, as the time for his accession to the throne grew ever closer. These gifts were the blocks which people used to build relationships with a future monarch, just as they were willing to make their houses over to his requirements. They wanted to feel that they were close to him, but he knew that no one could ever really be close to him. Not even his wife. For to be a king was essentially to be alone.

He glanced over at Millie and saw their host gave a small smile as he correctly interpreted Gianferro's wishes. 'Perhaps you would both care to see the library? Before lunch is served.'

To Millie's relief they were left alone—completely alone—and, frustrated with this no-man's land in which she found herself, she ran across the room into his arms, unable to stop herself.

She heard his breath quicken as he bent his head to kiss her, yet she sensed his restraint as she pressed her body closer to his. But she didn't care. Her senses had been awoken and she was greedy for his touch. For a moment she felt as though she had hit a button straight to paradise, as his mouth moved with such sweet intimacy over hers, but when she gave a little moan of delight he disentangled her—rather like someone restraining a sweet but rather over-eager puppy.

She turned bewildered blue eyes up to him. 'You don't want me any more?'

Gianferro frowned and quelled the desire deep inside him. How sweetly passionate she was! He was unused to such unfeigned enthusiasm, but he recognised that it was a double-edged sword. He must remember that there was a downside to her innocence, and he was going to have to teach her to school and to temper her desire. She must learn that he would always be the initiator of intimacy—unless in the privacy of the bedroom.

'You know I want you,' he murmured softly. 'But not here, and not now. Come and talk to me, Millie.'

'I *can't*,' she whispered. 'I feel out of my depth, and I don't know what is happening to me.'

'Don't you?' He took her by the shoulders and his eyes were fierce and black and burning. 'Have you not guessed why you are here?'

Millie shook her head. 'Not really.'

It was time. He drew a deep breath and his voice was both silken and yet commanding. 'You know that something was forged between us that day in the stable? Something I had not expected?'

'Nor wanted?' she guessed painfully.

The dark eyes became hooded. She must learn that introspection was an indulgence which brought with it only pain and no solution.

'What I want is an irrelevance—it is what I need which is at stake, and that was never in any doubt,' he said firmly. 'I have found what it is I am looking for.'

She felt as though she was poised on the edge of a precipice, staring down into a swirl of dark clouds, so that nothing before her was clear. But Millie's instincts were sound—and the most astonishing one was welling up inside her, even if she didn't quite dare to believe in it. She hesitated before she dared to voice it. 'Which is?'

'You,' he said quietly. 'I am going to marry you.'

She felt curiously flat. 'Aren't you suppose to ask me first?'

He gave a hard, almost brittle smile. Shouldn't he at least allow her the small fantasy of believing that she had some choice in the matter? That she had it in her to resist him when he had his heart set on something! 'Will you, Millie? Marry me?'

She didn't say anything.

'Your hesitation is good,' he observed softly. 'For it indicates that you understand the significance of what it is I am asking you.'

Millie put her fingers to her cheeks. She could feel

them flaming. 'But *m-marriage*?' she questioned shakily, her heart racing. 'Isn't a proposal supposed to follow—?'

'What?' His eyes were jet shards as he cut in, anticipating her next words. 'You imagine that I am able to offer you what other men would? A kiss goodnight on the doorstep? Trips to the theatre, perhaps? Or supper parties to meet mutual friends?' He took one hand from her face—her left hand—and turned it over in his, studying it thoughtfully. 'It can never be that way for me, Millie. When someone in my position chooses a bride, none of the normal rules of courtship apply.'

'You mean…you mean you're above the normal rules?'

'Yes,' he said simply, and it was not a boast—merely a statement of fact. 'If I meet you openly it will create a great media storm—not only here, but also in Europe—and it will compromise you. Public expectation will grow so intense that your every move will be monitored and recorded and the strain could become unbearable—I have seen it happen before. And for what purpose, Millie? When I know that you embody everything that I seek in a bride.'

'But why?' she questioned, still bewildered. 'Why me?'

'The truth?' She nodded, dimly aware that she might not like it. 'My requirements are simple. My bride must be pure, and she must be of aristocratic stock.'

Like one of the horses they had just seen, thought Millie, with a faint feeling of hysteria.

'You haven't taken lovers, and that is exactly how it should be.' His voice dropped to a sultry caress. 'And your first lover will surpass anything that any other man could ever offer you, that I can promise you.' Her blush pleased him, and excited him, too.

'But why not a Mardivinian woman?'

He shook his head. 'That would be too complicated, and I know all the possible candidates too well. There would be no sense of freshness among the women who would be suitable—and besides, my two sisters-in-law are English. They will provide you with the company you need to prevent you from becoming homesick. And your upbringing will have equipped you perfectly for the task which lies ahead.'

'Task?' she echoed.

He nodded. 'English women are brought up to be independent and resilient and resourceful—and your aristocratic background will enable you to mix with anyone, to understand how a future king will be brought up. For, as my Queen, you will bear my sons.'

Queen. The word hung in the air as if it had dropped into the conversation out of a fairytale. But this was definitely no fairytale—for if it had been then surely he would have mentioned the word that every bride-to-be the world over wanted to hear. Love. Millie stared into the proud, handsome face. She did not want words of love if he didn't mean them—and how could he possibly mean them when they barely knew one another, not really?

'Yet still you hesitate,' he observed softly, and he played his final winning card as he drifted her fingertips towards his lips and brushed them against the sensual lines with slow deliberation. He felt her shiver beneath his touch. 'Shall I tell you what is most important of all?' he questioned silkily.

'Y-yes,' she said breathlessly. 'Tell me.'

'This connection between us. It is strong. Powerful. It cannot be ignored. You feel it, too—you cannot deny it, can you, Millie?' His eyes were lit with triumph, but with something else, too. 'And so do I,' he finished on an afternote of bemusement.

'Yes,' she agreed boldly. 'I feel it, too.'

The blood drumming through her veins was threatening to deafen her and she nodded mutely, shivering with increased excitement as he lowered his head to tease her with the lightest and most provocative of kisses.

'See the way you make me feel…here.' And Millie nearly died when he guided her hand to his loins. She felt his hot, hard heat pressing against her, and some answering flame leapt up into life inside her, making her melt and making her ache. The sensation obliterated all others—including the one painful and fleeting thought that perhaps for Gianferro that was all there was. Chemistry. Sexual chemistry. And suitability.

'Yes,' he whispered exultantly as he saw her eyes

darken and her lips part, heard the breathless little whimper she made. 'Without this there can be nothing between a man and a woman. For all your innocence I desire you very much—perhaps more than I have ever desired a woman before, because never before have I had to wait. It shall be my body that you know, and mine alone. I shall tutor you in the ways of love and teach you how to please me as much as I will please you. You will be Queen of Mardivino and you shall have everything your heart desires. The finest racehorses will be yours for the asking. Jewels. Baubles. All the things that women crave are within your reach, Millie.'

She wanted to tell him that those things were not important, not in the grand scheme of things. That somehow he had ensnared her with a dark and silken certainty, capturing her heart to ensure that she would never be free of him—nor ever want to be free of him. 'Gianferro—'

'And I shall tell you something else,' he forged on relentlessly. 'If you do not accept me, then you will spend the rest of your life regretting it—for you will never meet another man of my equal. All men will be shadows in comparison, mocking you and taunting you with the thought of what might have been.'

If Millie had been older she might have damned him for his arrogance—but even with her almost laughable innocence she recognised the truth behind his words. Maybe she should have asked for more time, but time seemed as rare a commodity to him as privacy. She could do nothing but stare into the dark promise of his eyes, and as she did she felt her knees threaten to give way. She clutched onto him as if he was her anchor in a stormy sea. 'Gianferro!' she gasped. 'Please! Please! Won't you just kiss me?'

He hid his smile of satisfaction, for it was then that he knew she was his.

CHAPTER FOUR

UNSEEN, Millie put the tiny contraceptive Pill into her mouth and swallowed it—then walked into the bedroom, her face as white as the wedding gown which was hanging there. She shook her head from side to side. 'I don't know if I can go through with it, Lulu,' she said huskily.

'Stuff and nonsense!' said Lulu, giving the kind of brisk, no-nonsense smile which only big sisters could get away with. Especially big sisters who had only recently forgiven you for stealing their boyfriends. Her smile increased. 'As someone else once in pretty much my position quipped—your name's on the teatowels now, it's much too late to back out.'

And Lulu was right—it was. Her name and Gianferro's. Not just on teatowels either, but on teasets too—and splashed all over breakfast trays, and some specially minted coins—all carrying the same formal and rather rigid pose of her and Gianferro, which had been taken on the day that their engagement was announced to the world.

Bizarrely, she found herself wondering if Gianferro had ever even *used* a teatowel. She doubted it. Or cooked a meal for himself. Equally doubtful. Her own upbringing had been privileged, yes—but at least she and her sister had been Brownies with the local pack. She knew how to clean and how to cook, and how to produce a plate of squashy-looking cupcakes which people would buy for charity.

But not Gianferro.

With every day that passed she became more and more aware of the rarefied and very isolated world he inhabited. Getting to see him was fraught with difficulty—like trying to make an emergency appointment at the dentist. He was surrounded by aides, and one in particular—Duca Alesso Bastistella, a devastingly handsome Italian nobleman whom Lulu had confessed she could 'fall in love with at the drop of a hat'.

Well, Millie couldn't. Alesso was like a gate-keeper—oh, he was always smoothly charming and diplomatic, but he seemed to have almost permanent access to Gianferro, whilst denying it to everyone else.

'We were at school together and he is my right-hand man,' said Gianferro one day, when she questioned him on it. 'I trust him,' he added simply.

He made trust sound like a precious and rare commodity, and Millie wondered if it would ever be possible to befriend the powerful Alesso. Well, if she wanted to get close to her husband, she was going to have to try.

She tried not to get too down about it, but she could have counted on one hand the number of times she had been alone together with Gianferro, when he had teased her with kisses which had made her melt inside, imprinting his lips upon hers with sensual promises of the pleasures to come. Of course she understood that his father was gravely ill, and that there had to be amendments made to the Constitution because of the forthcoming wedding, but even so...

'And anyway,' said Lulu softly, 'you're off to the Cathedral in little under an hour, to make your wedding vows—so you couldn't back out of it even if you wanted to!'

'I know I am,' said Millie faintly, and went to sit down. But Lulu held up her hand like a traffic policeman.

'Be careful, or you'll crumple your lingerie!'

'There doesn't seem enough of it to crumple.'

'That's the whole point!' Lulu gave a foxy smile. 'Anyway, I want to do your make-up now, so come over here and sit beside the mirror. Carefully.'

At least she had made it up with her sister. Thank heavens. But then Lulu—for all her fiery temper—had never been one to bear a grudge. Once she had accepted that the wedding was going to happen whether she liked it or not, she had accepted it with good grace. Especially when she realised that she had the chance to be a bridesmaid.

'The *only* bridesmaid, I hope?'

'Well, there will be Gianferro's tiny niece, but you'll be the only adult one, yes.'

Since then, Lulu had been over the moon.

'Just think of all the people I'm going to meet!' she had sighed.

'But what about Ned?' Millie had queried.

'Ned who?' Lulu had laughed.

For the past month, since the engagement, Millie had been living in a 'small' house within the Palace grounds, with Lulu and her mother on hand to chaperone her. Not that their services had been needed for *that*, she thought somewhat resentfully as she stared at her bare face in the mirror. Gianferro was taking restraint to the extreme—for they had barely spent a moment on their own.

But all that would change after the wedding, she thought, as Lulu began to slap some sticky moisturiser onto her cheeks. That was what honeymoons were for—proper old-fashioned honeymoons—when a couple got to know each other in all the ways that mattered.

Would she be a good wife to him? Would instinct and the books she had been poring over help guide her in the bedroom department? A nervous shiver ran down her spine, and Lulu's hand halted in its process of dipping a damp sponge into some foundation.

'*Now* what's the matter?'

Millie bit her lip. 'Nothing.'

'Not worried about the sex bit, are you?' questioned Lulu perceptively.

Millie shook her head. She couldn't voice her fears—she just couldn't—not to anyone, and especially not to Lulu. If she started talking about it, then she would end up feeling—not for the first time—as if her purity was the *only* reason Gianferro was marrying her. And besides, there were some things which should remain private.

'Not a bit,' she said staunchly.

Lulu smiled. 'Pity you did all that horse-riding,' she commented.

'What's that supposed to mean?'

'Well, isn't there some kind of ancient ritual which demands you hang the bloodied sheet from the Palace windows?'

'Oh, *do* shut up, Lulu!' Millie closed her eyes. 'Have you seen the papers?'

'I thought you weren't going to read them any more.'

'I know I wasn't—but there's a certain irresistibility about it—like being told not to touch a hot plate in a restaurant—you immediately want to.'

There was nothing in the latest batch of publications which hadn't been there from day one. She had been dubbed the 'unaffected' aristocrat, which she gathered was newspaper-speak for someone who didn't know her way round a make-up bag. Or a wardrobe.

Thank heavens she had Lulu on-side—for it had been Lulu who had taken her on a grand tour of Paris's top couturiers in a search for the Perfect Wedding Dress. The procession of garments which had been paraded in front of them had made her know what she *didn't* want.

In the end Millie had bought the dress in England—all soft layers of tulle that floated like a ballerina's petticoats, much to Lulu's disgust.

'It looks like a meringue!' she had exclaimed. 'You looked far sexier in that silk-satin sheath.'

But brides weren't supposed to look sexy—they were supposed to look virginal and, in her case, regal. Millie knew that there were high expectations about the gown, and that it was her duty to meet them. Little girls would pore over pictures of it. They wanted a fairytale princess, and she would make sure they got one.

'Surely that's enough mascara?' she ventured anxiously.

'Can't have enough,' said Lulu, with one final sweep of the wand. 'Your eyes will come out much better in the photos if you slap it on—you'll look gorgeous.'

'Especially to the world's panda population,' said Millie weakly, as she slid on the hand-made pearl-encrusted shoes and then, at last, slithered into the dress itself.

'Oh, wow!' said Lulu softly, as she adjusted the soft tulle veil. 'Wow!'

Millie just stood and stared at herself in disbelief.

Was that really her?

The high collar made the most of her long neck, and the beaded sash emphasised her tiny waist. Tight white sleeves ran down into a point on her hands, and the skirt shimmered to the floor in a soft haze of filmy white.

It was just her face which took some getting used to. With the unaccustomed make-up transforming her eyes into Bambi-like dimensions, and the pale blonde hair coiled into an elaborate chignon to accommodate the heavy diamond tiara she would don after the vows, she didn't look like Millie at all. She looked… she looked…

'Like a *princess*,' breathed Lulu.

Please let me be a good one, prayed Millie silently as a servant gave a light rap at the door. She picked up her bouquet, taking a deep breath to calm herself. The Princess bit was only part of the deal—far more important was that after today she would legally be Gianferro's wife, and they would be together, and they would learn to grow and share within their marriage. An image of his dark-eyed face swam before her and her nervousness became brushed with the golden glimmer of excitement. Oh, but she wanted to be alone with him!

Not for the first time Millie found herself wishing that Gianferro was just a normal man, and that they were making their vows in the tiny village church near her home, where her own parents had married. That they were going back to Caius Hall afterwards for the wedding breakfast, instead of the Rainbow Palace—so vast that she felt like Alice in Wonderland every time she set foot inside it.

Yet her two English sisters-in-law seemed to have

adapted well to life as princesses—and they had both been commoners, without a drop of aristocratic blood in their veins. But they had been older, she reminded herself. And experienced. And the Princes they had married had not been future Kings…

Millie could feel the palms of her hands growing clammy as the ride to Solajoya's Cathedral passed as if in a dream. There seemed to be thousands of people out on the streets, and the flashbulbs of the photographers were so blinding and ever-present that the day seemed bathed in a bright, artificial light.

Her wedding gown and flowers had been left to her, but Gianferro had masterminded the rest of the wedding plans, and Millie had been happy for him to do so. She understood that there were certain rituals to be followed, and she understood the weighty significance of the ceremony itself. The world and Mardivino were watching, and the Cathedral was packed with Royals and dignitaries and Presidents and Prime Ministers.

She knew that there was a small knot of her own relatives and family friends close to the altar, but she could not make out a single familiar face—they all swam into one curious and seeking blur. Never in her life had she known such a sense of lonely isolation as she began to walk towards him.

Because her father was dead, there was no one to give her away. A long-lost uncle had been half-heartedly suggested, but rejected by Gianferro.

'No,' he had said decisively. 'You will come to me alone.'

The aisle seemed to go on for miles, as music from massed choirs spilled out in some poignantly beautiful melody. Millie clutched her bouquet just below waist level, as she had been told to, and there, by the flower-decked altar, stood the tall, dark figure of Gianferro.

She could not see his face—all she was aware of as she grew closer was that he was in some kind of uniform, and that he looked formidably gorgeous. But a stranger to her, with his medals, and his hat with a plumed feather tucked beneath his arm.

Now she could see him, his proud and unsmiling face. She searched the dark glitter of his eyes for some sign that his bride-to-be pleased him, and a frisson of fear ran through her. For a moment her sure and steady pace faltered.

Was that…surely that was not *displeasure* she read in his eyes?

For a moment Gianferro could scarcely believe what he was seeing—but it was not the customary pride and elation of a man looking at the woman he was about to marry, transformed into an angel with her wedding finery.

Ah, *si*, she was transformed. But…

Where were the unadorned pure features which had so captivated him? Her eyes looked so sooty that their deep blue beauty was lost, and the lips he had kissed so uninhibitedly were now slicked with a dark pink shade of lipstick. She looked like a…a…

His eyes narrowed. He was going to have to speak to her about that. She must learn about his likes and dislikes, and he detested heavy make-up. Yet his face gave nothing away as she reached his side—only the tiny pulse hammering at the side of his temple gave any indication of his disquiet—and he could do nothing to control that.

The hand she gave him was cold, but then Mardivino's Cardinal began to intone the solemn words, and all was forgotten other than the import of what he was saying.

As they emerged from the darkness into the brightness of the perfect summer's day, he turned his head to look down at her. She must have sensed it, for her moist eyes turned up to him, like a swimmer who had spent too long under water.

'Happy?' he questioned, aware that cameras were upon them, that video tapes would be slowed down and analysed, his words lip-read. A world desperate to know what he was really thinking, to hear what he was really saying. Gianferro had never known real privacy, and it was a hard lesson that Millie was going to have to take on board.

She felt the squeeze of his hand, which felt like a warning, and managed a tremulous smile. 'Very,' she replied. But she felt light-headed—the way you did when you'd had medication just before an operation, as if she had temporarily flown out of her own body and was hovering above it, looking down.

She saw her painted doll mask of a face, and the little-girl trepidation in the heavily mascaraed eyes. And then Gianferro was guiding her towards the open carriage—her tulle veil billowing like a plume of white smoke behind her, diamonds glittering hard and bright in the tiara which crowned the elaborate confection of hair.

The Rainbow Palace looked like a flower festival, and every step of the way there was someone to meet or to greet. Another person offering their bowing congratulations. Millie could see ambition written on the faces of the men who spoke to Gianferro, and narrow-eyed assessment from the women. Who was this bride their Crown Prince had brought to Mardivino? their expressions seemed to say.

Good point, thought Millie—just who am I?

She was beginning to despair of ever getting a moment alone with him—this outrageously handsome man who was now her husband—but at last they were seated side-by-side in the Banqueting Hall, dazzled by the array of gold and crystal.

He turned to her. 'So, Millie,' he said softly. 'The first hurdle has been crossed.'

She laughed. 'I can think in terms other than horse-riding, you know!' she hesitated. 'You...you haven't said whether you like my dress,' she said shyly.

'The dress is everything it should be.'

And? *And? Say I look beautiful, even if you don't*

mean it… For wasn't every bride supposed to look beautiful on her wedding day—just from radiance and excitement alone?

He dipped his head towards hers; she could feel his breath drifting across her skin. 'Why did you cover your face with so much make-up?'

Millie blinked, remembering Lulu's words. 'For the cameras, of course!'

He had chosen an innocent country girl—not some Hollywood starlet, concerned about her image above all else! His mouth flattened.

'You don't like it?' ventured Millie painfully.

He shook his head, trying to dispel the tight band which was clamped around his head. The strain of the last few weeks had been intense, but after the wedding breakfast they would be alone at last, and then, in slow, pleasurable time, he could show her exactly what *did* please him.

'Your skin is too fine too clog it up like that, *cara mia*,' he observed softly. He saw her lips begin to tremble at the admonishment and he laid his hand firmly over hers, olive skin briefly obscuring the new, shiny gold of her wedding band. His voice was little more than a whispered caress. 'Later you will scrub it off—do you understand? You will come to me bare and unadorned, stripped of all finery and artifice.' He felt the deep throb of desire, which he had put on hold for so long that it seemed like an eternity. Carefully he took his hand away, for touch could tempt even the most steely resolution. 'And that, *cara* Millie—*that* is how I wish to see you.'

With a tremulous smile she nodded, then accepted a goblet of champagne from one of the footmen with a gratitude which was uncharacteristic. Never had she needed the softening effect of alcohol quite so much, and she drank deeply from the cup. Her very first test as the future Queen and she had failed him!

She longed to rush out to the bathroom and wash it all off, there and then—but she would not dare to take such a liberty; new princesses did not nip off to powder their noses. In fact, from now on, her behaviour would have to be choreographed right down to the last second. The simple things which other people took for granted would be out of her reach. Even her mother had remarked drily, 'You'd better cultivate a strong bladder, Millie.'

'Smile for me now, Millie,' he instructed silkily, wishing to see those dark shadows pass from her eyes. 'And think instead what it will be like on our honeymoon.'

This was a thought which had made her alternate between giddy excitement and stomach-churning nerves in the run-up to the wedding, but now the champagne had dissolved away her misgivings, and she felt her heart well up with the need to show him how good a wife she would be to him.

She began to pleat her napkin, until she remembered that all eyes were upon them and stopped. 'You haven't told me yet where we're going,' she observed quietly.

His eyes glittered with ebony fire. 'Traditionally, is not the honeymoon supposed to be a surprise—a gift from the groom to his bride?'

She wanted to say that, yes, of course it was—but suddenly it seemed to represent a whole lot more than that. Because of tradition Gianferro had taken charge of the wedding, and she understood that, but couldn't he have bent tradition in a way that would not have mattered to anyone other than the two of them? To have told her their destination—or, better still, to have allowed her to help choose. She felt disconnected. Out of control. As if her life had become a huge stage and she had been given the tiniest walk-on role.

But she didn't want to start their marriage on the wrong foot. If she wanted to change the unimportant things in the status quo then it had to be a gentle drip-drip—not like a child, instantly demanding a new toy. Gianferro was not used to living with a woman, just as she was not used to living with a man, and compromises must be made—she knew that, her mother had told her so. And he would not be familiar with compromise. Instinctively she recognised that negotiation was not part of his make-up, neither as a man or a prince. It would be up to her to lead the way. To show by example.

She wanted to say all the right things—as if her careful words could wash away that look of displeasure she had seen on his face in the Cathedral. To start together from now—a shiny new surface on which their future could be drawn. 'Yes, of course it is!' she said brightly. 'I love surprises!'

Gianferro smiled, pleased with her reaction, suddenly wishing that he could take her into his arms and kiss her. Properly. But there would be time enough for that later. 'Then I must hope that mine lives up to your expectation,' he murmured.

His words licked at her, with dark and erotic promise, and suddenly Millie was assailed with nerves. Please let me be worthy of him, she prayed. Let me be a good lover to him.

Gianferro's eyes narrowed. 'Why do you frown, *cara* Millie?'

She pulled herself together. Now was not the time to bring up her sexual inexperience! 'I wish my father could have been here,' she said truthfully. 'And yours.'

He nodded and gave her a soft smile, pushing away his untouched wine and reaching for a glass of water instead. His father had been frail for so long now that he could scarcely remember the vigorous man who had governed Mardivino with such energy—hiding well his heartbreak when his beloved wife had died. And lately he had grown more gravely ill. A dark shadow passed over his heart, but ruthlessly he banished it.

'Ah, but they were both here in spirit,' he answered quietly, remembering the look of relief which had spread over his father's careworn features when he had taken Millie to meet him. 'And my father is over-joyed that I have chosen a bride at last. This marriage has pleased him enormously.'

'And…it pleases you, too, Gianferro?' she questioned, emboldened by the wine.

He smiled. She was to step into the role demanded of her, and it seemed that his instincts were correct. She was the perfect choice. 'My destiny has been fulfilled,' he murmured.

It wasn't quite the answer she had been seeking, but Millie supposed that it would have to do. Quelling the butterflies in her stomach, she sat back as Gianferro's brother stood up to make a toast to the new Princess.

CHAPTER FIVE

'So, do you approve, Millie?'

Millie smiled, wishing she could rid herself of these stupid nerves. Calm down, she told herself—you're not the only virgin bride on the planet!

'It's…it's beautiful,' she said softly.

The white stuccoed house stood in its own beautifully landscaped gardens, which eventually ran down to the most beautiful beach she had ever seen—its powdery white sand was studded with pretty, pale shells which contrasted against a sea of blinding blueness.

As a honeymoon destination it was perfect.

Except…

Well, for a start they had been greeted at the door by a butler, a housekeeper, two maids and a chef.

'A skeleton staff,' Gianferro had remarked carelessly.

Millie had grown up having staff around, yet—naïvely, perhaps—she had thought that their honeymoon might be the exception. But apparently not.

Inside the house a small table had been laid up for tea in the sitting room, and she sipped at the scented brew gratefully, but had little appetite for the tiny

61

sandwiches and feather-light cakes which accompanied it.

'You do not like to eat?' Gianferro frowned. He had wanted to do something to remind her of England, to make her feel at home.

Millie saw the look in his dark eyes and bit into a cucumber sandwich as if her life depended on it. 'I guess I'm just a little tired,' she explained carefully. 'All the excitement of the day.' And all the days leading up to it. And the restless nights...

Gianferro's eyes narrowed. 'Then let us go to our bedroom,' he instructed silkily.

So the moment had come at last.

Millie felt like a novice swimmer who had been put on the highest diving board as they made their way to a beautiful room containing a vast bed, and there was a valet, removing the last of their empty cases.

She smiled politely at the servant. When would they *ever* be left on their own?

There had been one brief moment when they had left the wedding breakfast to go and change, when it had been just the two of them, and Millie had stood shyly in Gianferro's suite of Palace rooms—hers, too now, of course—and looked at him.

He had read the plea in her eyes correctly, taken her veil off with care and then bent his head to kiss her, and the kiss had been like setting fire to a heap of dry twigs. She had eagerly wrapped her arms around his neck, opening her mouth beneath his seeking lips, and given a little yelp of pleasure until he had smiled and shaken his head slightly.

'*Cara,*' he had demurred, gently but firmly unwrapping the arms which clung to him. 'Not now. Not yet. And not here.'

'But…' Her blue eyes were wide with bewilderment. 'We're alone. We're married.' *And I want you.* 'Why not?'

He gave a little sigh, as much composed of regret as frustration at her lack of understanding. He glanced at his watch. 'Because our departure has been arranged right down to the last second. The car is timed to leave in half an hour—and after that all the journalists can go away and file their copy. The guests cannot leave until we do—and I cannot leave Premiers and Presidents cooling their heels while I make love to my new wife!'

Millie flushed. 'Of course not. How stupid of me!'

'Do not worry. You will learn.' With the tips of his fingers he tilted her face upwards. 'There will be time enough for the pleasures of the bedroom, Millie. And I do not intend our first time to be a quick…' His eyes glittered. 'How do they say? A ''wham-bam'', followed by a hurried dressing which would arouse the knowing smirks of Palace staff.'

Mille's colour deepened even further. She didn't want a quick 'wham-bam' either—whatever *that* was! She had hoped for passion and for spontaneity—but now she saw that those hopes were incompatible with her new status.

A great wave of panic began to swell up inside her, but with an effort she wished it away again. Stop fretting, she told herself. It will be all right.

But she was trembling as she turned her back on him, feeling so strange standing there in her pure white wedding gown. 'Would you mind…unzipping my dress?'

He opened his mouth to call for the new dresser he had appointed for her, but thought better of it, instead sliding the zip slowly all the way down to the small of her back. How tiny her waist! And just above where the zip ended was a peep of the transparent lace of her panties. He swallowed as temptation washed over him, and began to unbutton his uniform.

'There,' he said thickly. 'You can manage now.'

She buried herself in activity—scuttling into the bathroom in her bra and panties, feeling overwhelmingly shy as his dark and impenetrable gaze followed her. She took care to wipe most of the offending make-up from her face and, once she had removed the tiara, tugged all the constricting pins from her hair and brushed it free. Then she slipped on the dress and hat which had been chosen as her going-away outfit.

'How's that?' she asked as she reappeared.

He gave a slow and lazy smile. A pink voile dress, cream shoes and a large cream picture hat, trimmed with blowsy pink silk roses which looked almost real. Her blonde hair was a pale waterfall which gleamed over her shoulders and emphasised the youthful bloom of her skin. She looked like a picture from an old-fashioned book. *'Perfetto,'* he applauded softly. 'My beautiful and innocent English rose!'

And Millie smiled back with relief.

Gianferro's brothers had tied metallic balloons to the open-top car, and Princess Lucy had scrawled 'Just Married!' in deep vermilion lipstick on the bonnet of the expensive car!

But there were outriders, too, and shadowy figures in a car which sat on their tail as they moved away.

Millie had thought that they would all disappear once they had driven through the cheering crowds and out of the capital, but they were still there as the powerful vehicle began to ascend the mountain road.

She glanced behind her. 'They're not coming with us, are they?' she said, only half-joking, but she had her answer in the slight pause before he answered.

'Naturally.'

She opened her eyes very wide. 'They are?'

'They are my bodyguards, Millie,' he said quietly. 'Where I go, they go, too.'

All the conflicting emotions of the day made her feel light-headed enough to blurt out the first thing which came into her head.

'I presume they won't be joining us in the bedroom?'

Gianferro's mouth hardened. Well, what did she expect? Really? 'Of course not,' he answered coldly.

It was a variation of the look he had given her in the Cathedral—displeasure. Another person might have hidden it.

But another person would not have been Crown Prince! Who had spent all his life having his wishes acceded to, his moods catered for. Why should he bother hiding something? More importantly, how was she intending to handle it, as his wife? She with no experience of any man at all?

Maybe that was better. Her slate was clean and ready to be written on. There was no murky history to look back over, to compare with what was happening to her now, with him. They were starting over, and if she wanted an intimacy with him which she suspected had been completely lacking in his life, then she must let him show her how. It could not be done in a minute, or even a day—but slowly, bit by bit.

She would not be offended if he was cool with her! Instead she would ignore it, find a way to work round it. And if she encountered a rock in the path which led to their happiness, then she would simply step over it!

She smiled with delight now, as she looked round at their luxurious honeymoon bedroom, where roses and lilies were crammed into priceless vases, scenting the air with their incomparable perfume.

'That is better,' he murmured with approval as he saw her face. The door closed softly behind the valet and his gaze briefly flickered over to it, his lips curving into an answering smile. 'And what would you like to do now?' he questioned softly.

Millie blushed, not daring to tell him how much

she wanted him to take her in his arms again. For all she knew another servant would come bouncing into the room, or there might be something else they were supposed to be doing. 'I have no idea,' she said shyly.

He took her by the shoulders, his eyes now burning black fire and glittering with a certain kind of mischeviousness, too. 'You don't?' he teased. 'Millie, I'm disappointed in you!'

'Gianferro—'

'Shh!' He lowered his lips to tease them against hers in a light, brushing kiss and felt her breath escape in a low rush of pleasure. 'Ah! Yes! Yes, I know. It has been so long.'

Millie sank against him, her eyes fluttering to a close as she felt sensation begin to close her off from the world. 'Too long,' she sighed.

'Shall I close the shutters?'

Her eyes snapped open. 'But…but won't the bodyguards see? Won't they know what we're doing?'

He touched her long hair with an affectionate gesture. 'You think that we will only be permitted to make love once night has fallen and the guards have retired for the night?'

'I don't *know*.'

He continued to stroke the silken strands. 'My position dictates that I must be protected from threat— which means that my bodyguards must never be far away,' he explained slowly. 'But their position also dictates that they know their place, and now that place is to turn a blind eye to what happens. We shall not have the freedom of other honeymoon couples, Millie—I cannot, for example, make love to you on the edge of the shore, while the waves rock us with their own particular rhythm.' He smiled as he saw the startled look on her face. 'But we can create whatever fantasy we wish within this house. I think you will find that we do not need the stimulation of the out-doors or the lure of the forbidden—for us to travel to paradise.'

His words were a catalyst to the yearning which had been growing and growing inside her since the very first time he had kissed her and branded himself upon her heart and her body.

'Will you show me how?' she questioned shyly.

It was probably the most erotic thing that anyone had ever said to him—but he was aware that its allure lay in its innocent rarity.

He felt his blood thicken, quicken. 'Oh, yes,' he breathed, as he threaded his fingers luxuriantly in the golden silk. 'I shall show you everything. By the end of our honeymoon you will know as much as any courtesan, Millie.'

Sometimes his words frightened her—like now—for they hinted at his past and mocked her for her own innocence. And she realised that, while she might be the pupil, she had to assert some of her own authority. She would not wait—mute and malleable as a puppet—while he called all the shots. For surely he would bore with always being the one to crack the whip?

'Stop talking,' she said urgently. 'Kiss me. Properly.'

The contrast between her inexperience and her eagerness was like a starting pistol firing deep in his groin. All the pent-up desire he had buried for so long licked into life and he bent his head once more. Only this time it was not a light, grazing kiss, but deeper, drugging, soft and hard all at the same time, and filled with sensual purpose.

'Oh!' cried Millie, and this time he did not stop her when her arms reached up for him. She felt her lips begin to open and flower as mouth explored mouth with the excitement of a child being presented with a beautiful box and being told that, yes, she could open it.

He reached to cup her breast in his palm, could feel its small swell grow heavy, the nipple begin to point, and he circled his thumb round and round it, her soft moans of pleasure making him want to rip the dress from her body and bury his mouth there instead.

But he must take it slowly. Her initiation was important; it would affect how she viewed sex for the rest of her life. She had waited and he had waited, and their patience must be rewarded with a long and lavish feast.

He skated the flats of his hands down over her narrow hips, then changed direction, letting one lie with indolent possession over the barely perceptible curve of her stomach. He felt her move restlessly and he gave a low and predatory laugh as he moved, drifting his fingers between the fork of her legs and then drifting them away again.

'Oh!' she gasped automatically—the one word torn from her lips in a muffled protest.

'Oh, what?' he questioned lazily, still drifting his finger back and forth, back and forth.

But she couldn't speak, couldn't think—her heart was thumping so forcefully that all she could do was nod her head, terrified by the strength of the feelings which were scorching the nerve-endings of her body, and yet terrified that they might simply go away again.

'I think it is time that we took your dress off, don't you, Millie?'

With a practised, almost careless touch, he peeled the voile gown from her body and threw it aside, and then he stood back to look at her, appraising her scantily clad body as a connoisseur might appraise a painting.

Standing before him in just her underwear, Millie should have felt shy, but something in the increased darkening of his eyes filled her with a new and strange kind of power. For, yes, Gianferro was the expert, the seasoned lover, but she had something that he wanted as badly as she did.

Instinct, as well as skill, had made her a fearless and accomplished horsewoman, and instinct took over now to instruct her in the lessons of love. She raked her fingers up by her ears, lifting great handfuls of shiny gold hair, as if she were gathering sheaves of wheat, and the movement made her hips jut out slightly and emphasised the thrust of her breasts.

He sucked in a breath. 'Beautiful.' He slowly ran the tip of his finger down over his shirt. 'Come and unbutton this for me.'

It was the simplest task imaginable, but never had a task seemed so impossible. Gianferro smiled as she fumbled at the buttons.

'No need to ask whether you've done this before,' he teased.

'Don't make fun of me,' she begged.

'But I'm not. I never would.' His voice was serious because inexplicably he was moved. 'It's wonderful. Your innocence is all that a man could dream of.'

She pushed away the thought that it was what she represented, rather than the person she was, which made his black eyes gleam with such a soft, territorial pride, and concentrated instead on the newness and the excitement of the moment.

She'd never seen his chest before. It was olive-brown and silken satin in texture, crisp with dark hair, the faint line of rib barely visible. She touched a wondering finger to each nipple, then looked up at him to see his face a study of fierce concentration, as if he was holding himself back. His eyes opened again and he gave a little shake of his head, a smile which was almost rueful.

'Come,' he said huskily. 'For I cannot wait much longer.' And he scooped her up into his arms and carried her to the vast bed, which both taunted and tempted her as he laid her down on it and slid the shirt from his powerful shoulders.

He kicked off his shoes and, enraptured, Millie watched as he unbuckled his belt and slid the zip down. But she closed her eyes when the trousers came off, for she could see the proud, hard ridge through the silk of his boxer shorts.

'Open them, Millie,' he instructed quietly. 'Do not be afraid of what you see, for a man and a woman were made for each other. You know that.'

Yes, she did—and she had spent a lifetime of watching this most basic of acts in the stables, and in the farms surrounding her home in England. But animals were different from humans. Animals just got on and did it—you didn't get a mare standing there and hoping against hope that she would please her stallion!

'It will be fine,' he said sternly, but there was a mocking and teasing note to his next words. 'It *will* be fine—for I command it and you must obey all my commands!' She laughed then, and he pulled her against him. 'That is better. We will not rush. We have all the time in the world, *cara mia*.'

He had never known what it was to use restraint in the bedroom, for he had been spoiled by women all his life—women eager for his hard, beautiful body and for the cachet of having slept with a prince.

But Millie was different. His wife and his virgin. He must be gentle with her, but above all he must show her just how good it could be.

She had thought that it would be happening by now. She had thought... But then he began to kiss her again, and she just slipped into the beauty of that kiss, all her doubts and questions dissolving away.

He touched her skin with fingertips which whispered over the surface, and where he touched he set her on fire with need, like a painter, bringing to life a blank canvas with the stroke of his brush. Yet he touched her everywhere except where the books had told her she could expect to be touched, and this had the curious effect of both relaxing her and yet making the tension grow and grow.

Tentatively she stroked him back, tiptoeing her way over the landscape of his body, exploring and charting all the lines and contours. But there was an area which was out of bounds, for she didn't dare...

Against her lips she felt him smile, and he pulled his head away. 'That's okay, Millie—I actually do not want you to touch me there.'

The fact that he had guessed mortified her, but her confusion increased. 'You don't?'

'If you play with me, I will not do you justice.'

'I'm not a meal, to be eaten!' she protested.

'Oh, but you are,' he demurred, tempted to show her—but experience told him not to swamp her with too much, too soon. The first time should be unadorned—the myriad of variation on that one simple act should be revealed slowly, in time.

Soon she was aching, melting, longing—and when she thought she might die with it he took her bra off and peeled down her panties, touching the searing heat between her legs until she cried out.

Wild and hungry for him, her fears and doubts fell by the wayside and she boldly touched him back, feeling him start as she encountered the steely column.

He nodded, as if she had pressed some invisible button, and peeled off his boxer shorts. She felt the naked power of him butting against her, dimly aware that he was moving on top of her. She laid her hands on his buttocks and felt him shudder as he shifted position slightly and then...then...

'Millie!' he gasped, as he eased his way inside her. So tight! So perfect!

And Millie gasped, too. The newness of the sensation felt so strange and yet so right, as her body adjusted to accommodate him. Her skin felt flushed. All her senses felt as though they were newly sensitised. And her heart felt as though it wanted to burst from her chest as he sealed the union with a kiss which felt far more intimate than any previous kiss had done.

He began to move, slowly at first, dragging his mouth away to look down at her, his eyes narrowing—for he realised that just as this was new for her, in some ways it was the same for him. 'I am hurting you?'

She shook her head, and a laugh bubbled up from the back of her throat. It was so easy. 'No! Oh, no, not at all! It's...perfect...'

He shook his head. 'Not yet. Be patient, and you will see how perfect it can be.'

And then there were no more words or questions as their bodies melded and moulded and began to move in sweet harmony. Sometimes he teased her, and sometimes he thrust so deep that her heart felt as though it had been impaled by him, and all the time there was something tantalising, sweet and intangible, which was building and building inside. Over and over she felt that she was almost there, and her body reached for it greedily, but Gianferro did speak then, bending his mouth to whisper into her ear.

'Relax. Let go. Let it happen.'

When it did, she was unprepared for the power of it. And the beauty.

'G-Gianferro!' she gasped in astonishment as it took her up, lifted her in its nebulous arms like a whirlwind, and then rocked her, again and again, sucking all the air from her lungs until she fell at last, laughing and crying with the sheer wonder of it.

He stilled for a moment as he watched her—the genuine joy of her fulfilment touching him in a way he had not expected—and then he started to move again, and her eyes flew open. She read something in his eyes and she put her hands around his buttocks, pulling him in closer, deeper.

And when it happened for him she watched him too—drinking in his face greedily as she imprinted each reaction on her memory. She saw his eyes close, his head jerk back. A moment of rigidity, before he moaned, the sound of surrender being torn from the back of his throat. And when he opened them again, he seemed almost dazed, murmuring something softly in Italian.

Millie propped herself up on one elbow to look at him, her hair falling all over her shoulders as she studied his face. But the dazed look had disappeared, replaced by the harder, guarded and more familiar expression.

But Millie had seen it. For a moment or two he had been—yes, *vulnerable*—not something you would usually associate with him. She wondered if it was the same for all men—whether they opened up just a little and allowed you to see the softer side of them. And was it only after making love?

'What was that you said?' she questioned.

He shook his head. 'Nothing.'

Millie pulled a face. 'Oh, that's not fair, Gianferro! You can't use your fluency in other languages to exclude me.'

'Can't I?' he challenged softly, his words light and teasing, but she recognised that he meant them. 'Perhaps what I said was not suitable for a woman to hear.'

This was even worse. 'I may have been innocent,' she protested, 'but I'm not any more! I want to learn—and how better can I learn the secrets of the bedroom than from my husband?' Her mouth curved into a smile. 'I want to please you.'

'But you do.'

'And I want to enlarge my knowledge,' she added firmly.

He gave her a rueful look and pulled her into his arms. 'I was voicing my surprise and my pleasure because it is exactly as other men say it is.'

Millie frowned, not understanding at all.

'To make love without protection,' he elaborated. 'To ride bareback, as I believe the Americans call it.' He saw her colour heighten. 'You see!'

But Millie was shaking her head, trying to make sense of what he was saying. 'You mean…you mean you've never made love to a woman without…' She hesitated over the word—new to her, like so much else. '*Protection* before?'

He seemed astonished that she should have asked. 'But, no! Never!'

'Because…because of the risk of disease?' she ventured.

'Of course.' He nodded, picking up her fingers and kissing them, his breath warm and his smile full of satisfaction. 'And there are no such risks with you, *cara mia*. But it is far more than that…you see, my seed carries within it the bloodline of Mardivino, and it cannot be spilled carelessly!'

On the one hand it was a very old-fashioned and poetic way of putting it, and yet it was mechanical, too—as if she was nothing other than a very clean vessel. Millie bit her lip.

'I told you you would not like it,' he said softly as he observed her reaction.

But it wasn't that. It was the way his voice had

grown so stern when he had mentioned his bloodline. She realised that they still hadn't got around to discussing contraception. He must have just assumed that she would get herself sorted out before the wedding, as everyone had advised her to do.

She snuggled up against him. 'Don't you think that there are a few things we ought to talk about?'

'Before or after I make love to you again?' he questioned, his voice silky with erotic promise, and Millie shivered in anticipation as she felt the hardening and tensing of his body.

She closed her eyes as he began to touch her breasts. 'I guess...I guess it can wait,' she said shakily.

This time there was a sense of urgency, but there was a question burning inside her, too, as Millie wondered if it could possibly be as good again.

She was still a novice, but already she had learnt. Already she was comfortable with his body, and this time she was not afraid to touch him as freely as he did her. She saw his fleeting look of surprise, quickly followed by one of pleasure as their cries shuddered out in unison.

Oh, yes, she thought happily. Just as good. She stretched luxuriously. No. Better.

He turned to face her, a flush highlighting the aristocratic cheekbones and the hectic glitter of satisfaction in his black eyes giving no indication of the bombshell he was about to drop.

'So, *cara*,' he drawled softly, 'do you think we have made you pregnant?'

CHAPTER SIX

FOR a moment, Millie froze—her body as motionless as a stone—yet her mind raced with a speed which was frightening.

She played for time. 'Wh-what did you say?'

He smiled, but his voice was edged with a kind of territorial anticipation. 'I was thinking aloud, *cara*,' he murmured. 'Wondering whether even now my child begins to grow within your belly.'

She forced herself not to be swayed by the—again—poetic delivery of his words, but to concentrate instead on the implication which lay behind them.

She gave a strained smile. 'You…you wouldn't want me to be pregnant right now, would you?'

'But of course!' His eyes narrowed and he frowned. 'Marriage is for the procreation of children. That is its primary function, in fact.' He gave a glimmer of a smile which only partly defused the sudden sense of terror she felt. 'Particularly in my case, *cara* Millie.'

My case, she noted. Not our. But she must keep calm. She must. Obviously they weren't going to see eye to eye on every topic, not straight away. Marriage was also about compromise, she reminded herself. And negotiation.

'I was sort of…hoping that we might have some time together first…getting to know one another,' she ventured. 'Before children come along.'

He pulled her against him, loving the way that the silk of her hair clothed her chest like a mantle, beginning to stroke it almost absently. 'Perhaps we will,' he mused. 'But the decision is not ours to take.'

Millie opened her eyes very wide. 'It isn't?'

'Of course not! The conception of our child is outside our control! It lies in the domain of a power far greater than ourselves.'

This was the moment to tell him. The moment to announce the fact that her doctor had prescribed her six months worth of the contraceptive Pill to be going along with.

But something stopped her, and Millie wasn't quite sure what it was.

Fear that he seemed to have everything so mapped out? Or fear that she had taken a step which instinctively she knew he would disapprove of?

If she told him, she could imagine him—perhaps after again expressing his displeasure—tossing the Pills away in a macho kind of way before making love to her again. And then what would happen? Well, you wouldn't need to be a biologist to work that one out. She might fall pregnant. Immediately.

Millie tried to imagine what that would be like— and the thought of it filled her with horror. Everything else was so startlingly new—Mardivino, being married, getting used to being a princess. How on earth could she cope if she threw motherhood into the equation?

Perhaps she could slowly work round to it…make him see things from her point of view. That there was nothing wrong with waiting for a while…that was what most couples did.

Idly, she trickled her finger around one of the whorls of dark hair on his chest and saw him give a nod of satisfaction. 'It would be nice to have a little time on our own first,' she observed drowsily. 'Wouldn't it?'

She must learn lessons other than those of the bedroom, thought Gianferro. Did she think that they were to become one of those couples who shared *everything*, as was the modern trend? Who were together from dawn to dusk? He repressed a slight shudder. Even if his position had not ruled that out, it was an option he would have run a million miles from anyway. 'That is what honeymoons are for, *cara*,' he said lightly.

'But we're only on honeymoon for a fortnight!' Millie protested.

He wondered if she had any idea of just how privileged she was to have a whole two weeks of his uninterrupted company. Of the planning that had gone into absenting himself from his duties as Crown Prince. Perhaps she should learn *that*, too.

'My life is a very busy one, Millie.'

'And I want to share it with you!'

Again, he bit back the urge to tell her that what she wanted was a foolish desire which would never come true. Nor ever could. To soften the blow—this would be a lesson for *him*, too. He was used to dictating his terms, to doing exactly as he pleased and having people fall in and accede totally to his wishes. But he recognised that to make this marriage a comfortable one he must learn to use tact and diplomacy.

'But you *will* be sharing it,' he said firmly. 'As my wife and as the mother of my children.'

For a moment she was scared again. It was as if she had taken a leap back by half a century. If not yet barefoot then certainly pregnant as soon as possible—if Gianferro had his way.

'Just that?' she questioned quietly.

'Of course not,' he answered silkily. 'There will be so much more to your life than that, Millie.'

She couldn't quite stop the shaky breath of relief. 'There will?'

'Naturally. You will not be tied by children—because, just as in your own childhood, there will be plenty of staff to look after them.'

But Millie's heart did not leap for joy at the thought of handing the care of her children to other people. Quite the contrary when she remembered her own experience, and especially the brief period when she had gone to the local school before being sent off to boarding school. It was there that she had realised for the first time that her life was different from other people's.

How vividly she remembered the empty ache inside when her classmates had been met by their mothers at the school gates instead of an uncaring au pair or stony-faced nanny. And even more poignant had been the stories they used to relate—of mothers who bathed them and made cakes for them, and fathers who played with them, taught them how to swim and climb a tree. She had only ever seen her parents at bedtime, when she was all washed and in her pyjamas to say goodnight—and sometimes not even then. Did she really want that for her own children? And times had changed…even for Royal families. Wouldn't Gianferro long to have a closeness with his offspring which had never been there for him?

'It might be nice to be a little bit hands-on with them,' she suggested lightly.

Gianferro kissed the tip of her nose. 'That will not, I think, be either possible or desirable. Our children will be brought up the way of all Royal children. And besides, you will not have time.' His dark eyes crinkled. 'There will be many charitable institutions which will require your patronage. Do not worry, sweet Millie—there will be plenty to keep you busy.'

It was a horrible phrase. *Keep you busy*. It implied that she would be filling in time, instead of embracing it fully, and it was worrying, for it was not how she imagined her future to be.

'I see,' she said slowly.

Gianferro could hear her faint note of disapproval and he frowned. How demanding women could be! She might be young and unspoiled but, like all women, she required symbols of her position in his life. Not diamonds, in her case, but...

'And we must not forget your horse, of course,' he said softly, with the air of a man who had pulled a rabbit out of a hat.

Millie blinked. 'My horse?'

The corners of his mouth edged upwards into a small smile of satisfaction which accompanied the sudden anticipatory gleam of pleasure in his black eyes. 'I told you that you would have the finest mount money can buy, and so you shall, Millie. I had intended to keep it as a surprise, but since you are obviously dissatisfied—'

'But I'm not—'

He cut through her protest as if she hadn't spoken. 'Then I see no reason to keep you in suspense. During the second week of our honeymoon I intend to take you to my stables on the western side of the island— which are world-class, incidentally.'

'Yes, I've heard of them,' said Millie, in a small voice.

'And there you shall choose a horse to bring back to the Rainbow Palace with you.' He watched her carefully, for her reaction was not the one he had been expecting. He knew how much she loved horses—so why was she not flinging her arms about his neck and thanking him? Did she not realise the honour he was according her? Why, there were top breeders who would give up everything they possessed to own one of the horses he was offering her! 'You are not pleased with the idea, Millie?'

She heard the coolness in his voice and attempted to redress the balance. She couldn't expect him to understand her doubts and her fears, and to express them would sound like whining defeatism. If you took the Royal part out of their situation, it helped put things in perspective. Because when it boiled down to it they were just two adults starting out on married life together—and communication was vital if the journey was to be a rich and fulfilling one. 'No, I am pleased—I'm delighted, if you want the truth, Gianferro!'

She was going to have to tell him about the Pill. He wasn't a Neanderthal—he was a sophisticated man of the world. And, yes, he might have a perfectly understandable desire to give Mardivino an heir—but surely he was also reasonable enough to be prepared to wait…even for a few months?

'Gianferro—'

'I know.' He anticipated her next words. 'You are worried about riding while with child, and I share your fears. I think that as soon as you become pregnant the riding will have to be curtailed until after the birth—no matter what the current thinking is! But abstinence only increases the hunger—and when you finally get back in the saddle it will be with an even greater excitement, that I can guarantee.'

He smiled, recalling his own self-imposed abstinence. The sacrifices he had made! He had not taken
a lover for over a year—it had seemed morally wrong
when he was actively seeking a bride. And of course
once he had found one he had felt morally bound to
continue, enduring the test on his sensual appetite as
he waited until after the wedding. He stroked Millie's
breast and felt her shiver. The wait had been well
worth it!

Millie lay there, listening to his words with a
mounting feeling of disbelief and panic. He had it all
worked out. No compromise, no negotiation at all.
And it pained her to admit it, but she knew that it
was true…there was no *room* for negotiation in
Gianferro's mind. He knew what he wanted and he
intended to have it. And he expected her to be grateful
for a couple of months of riding before she faded even
more into the background of his life once he had
made her pregnant!

But she was in the situation now, and it was pointless to try to rail against him on a subject which was
clearly so important to him and on which he clearly
would not budge. He wanted an heir and she was
perfectly happy to give him one. Just not yet. What
harm could it do if she waited a while? Lots of couples had to wait before a baby came. Why, they would
get lots and lots of practice!

Millie felt her body respond as he continued to
stroke her, the clamour of her senses smoothing down
the sharp edges of panic in her mind. They would get

close this way, she told herself. Closer and closer, until all the barriers fell.

She closed her eyes, and Gianferro felt a brief moment of triumph as he bent his head to kiss her. Had he not chosen her as much for her malleability as for her true innocence? She would learn that he would make the decisions—indeed was compelled to. That he knew best—for how could it be any other way, given the disparity in their individual experiences of the world?

Millie gasped as his mouth moved from lips to breast, his tongue flicking out to tease the hardening bud, and she clasped his dark head against her as pure pleasure shafted through her body.

He raised his head with a wicked smile which made her forget that he was a prince. Made her forget everything.

'Do you like that, Millie?' he murmured softly.

'It's...' Millie swallowed, finding it overwhelming to cope with all these new feelings—both physical and emotional. Her response was forgotten as he moved his head down to her belly. And then beyond. 'Gianferro!' she gasped, as shock mingled with pure ecstasy.

He tasted her with pleasure, the squealing uninhibitedness of her response only adding to his own hunger, and as he felt her spasm and dissolve against his tongue he fleetingly thought how wonderful it was going to be. He would be the only man she would ever know—her skills would be honed for just him!

Afterwards, they lay silently for a while, and then Gianferro yawned. 'We'd better think about getting ready for dinner,' he murmured.

She snuggled against him. 'I'm not hungry.'

'Well, I am.'

'Oh!' She wriggled even closer to him, feeling as though she'd found paradise here in his arms and unwilling to relinquish it, even for a second. 'Can't we just have something in bed?'

Gently but firmly he disentangled her arms from where they lay, wrapped around his hips. 'Unfortunately, no, *cara*. The chef will have gone to some trouble to prepare something special for our first night here, and we are obliged to eat it.'

Obliged. The word jumped out at her, reminding her of what Royal life was all about. Millie sighed. 'Of course. How silly of me not to have thought of that.'

'Indeed.' He nodded with satisfaction. 'And the sooner we eat it, the sooner the staff can be dismissed.' His voice dipped into a provocative caress. 'And the sooner we can come back to bed!'

The anticipation of *that* made her misgivings seem inconsequential. For a moment she felt like the old Millie—even if the memory of her was becoming more hazy by the second. Or at least she felt a bit more comfortable in the skin of the *new* Millie... though she was even *more* of a stranger. But the other Millie had been a girl, and now she was most definitely initiated into the ranks of womanhood. 'But we've spent most of the afternoon in bed!' she teased.

He relaxed as he saw her eyes shine. 'I know,' he agreed softly, and for one rare and blessed moment he felt completely at ease. He bent his mouth to her ear. 'And I intend to spend many more afternoons in exactly the same place!'

As Millie dressed for dinner she deliberately squashed the thought that she was deceiving him. She was *not*. She was acting in their best interests, and for the future of their relationship. And hadn't her mother told her that it was wise to always keep something back? That mystery added to a woman's allure...

But dinner was another trial—and Millie was no stranger to lavish dinners. Opposite sat her brand-new husband—looking dark and unruffled and cool in an open-neck cream silk shirt which gave a glimpse of the tantalising arrowing of dark hair beneath. His skin was olive and gleaming and he looked completely sensual and irresistible. He had lain naked in her arms, he had been joined with her in the most intimate way that a man and woman could be—so why, looking at him now, did that seem almost impossible to imagine?

The staff who served the meal spoke very little, but when they did it was in French or Italian, and Millie had rather neglected languages at school. For a moment she thought of Lulu. Lulu was effortlessly fluent in French, and if it had been her sitting here—as originally intended—she would no doubt have had all the staff smiling sunnily at her.

'Merci beaucoup,' she said, when their coffee was brought, and saw her husband give a small smile as the butler left the room. 'Oh, Gianferro—my French is terrible!' she wailed.

'It will improve.'

'I shall take lessons.'

'Indeed.' He nodded. 'I will find you a tutor.'

Millie hesitated. 'I was hoping perhaps I could go to a class with other people?'

Imperious dark brows elevated. 'Other people?'

'You know…' Millie shrugged her shoulders awkwardly. 'Like a regular class, or something. You must have them in Solajoya.'

'Of course we do. Our education system is one of the finest in the world.' Thoughtfully he ran a long olive finger over a glass of pure crystal. 'Though in your case it may not be appropriate.'

Millie blinked. 'Oh?'

'I do not hold with the idea of Royalty being accessible,' he observed quietly.

She thought she heard a warning note in his voice. 'You mean you want me to be…remote?'

'That is not the word I would have chosen.' He dropped a lump of sugar into one of the tiny gold-lined cups and stirred. When he looked up again his dark eyes were serious. 'You will need to be one step removed from your people—a part of them and yet apart from them. As if you were standing in the next-door room. Knock down the wall which divides you, and you run the danger of the roof caving in.'

Millie nodded, her thoughts troubled once more. All these things lay ahead. Such big things. Babies who would be heirs and a crown which was destined to be hers. With this dark and intelligent man by her side, whom she yearned to know better. But would she—when he was a self-confessed champion of being…not remote…but removed? She drank some coffee. She would persist. Whittling away at the barrier with which he surrounded himself. Some things could only be accomplished over time—and at least she had that on her side.

But the getting-to-know-him-properly bit had to start some time. She looked into his face—such a dark and forbidding face—except when he was making love, of course. She shook her head slightly, still filled with that slight sense of disbelief of what they had been doing together not so long ago.

A faint smile curved Gianferro's lips. 'Why do you blush so, Millie?' he questioned softly.

'I was just thinking…'

'Mmm?'

She heard the indulgent note in his voice—as if she was a child to be humoured. Would it sound unattractively naïve if she tried to tell him just how much of a woman he had made her feel in bed, but that now they were out of it all her glowing self-assurance seemed to have fled? Maybe it would be better to stick to basics. To start to get to know him in a way she had not previously been able to.

'What was it like,' she began, 'growing up on an island?'

He curved his finger around the warm coffee cup. 'In what respect?' he questioned carelessly.

Was she imagining the evasive note in his voice? Millie gave him a shy smile. Forget he's a prince, she told herself. Just ask him the kind of things you'd ask any man. But that was the trouble. She had no experience—not just of the bed bit, but all the other stuff which went to make up a relationship. In a way, the bed bit was easy—like learning to ride a horse. There were certain actions and movements you had to master—and after that it was up to you to modify and improve them.

But talking was harder. She had had none of the normal exposure to male/female interaction which most young women of her age had. No brothers, for a start, and then a single-sex school. There had been no nightclubs and precious few parties. Her life had been centred around the countryside and her horses— and that, of course, was one of the reasons he had made her his bride.

'Well, did you go to school?'

'My brothers and I were educated within the Palace.'

'That must have been quite…well, quite limiting, really.'

He raised his eyebrows. 'Not really. You went to

a boarding school, didn't you? That's a closed environment in itself.'

'But at least there were lots of other girls there.' Millie stared down at her cooling coffee and then looked up into his eyes once more. They were blacker than the inky coffee and they gave absolutely nothing away. Was that how he had been conditioned to look—as enigmatic as any Sphinx? Had he been trained to keep his feelings hidden—rigorously conditioned into not letting anyone have an inkling of his thoughts? Or was that just his own particular make-up? She smiled, sensing that she needed to soften her questioning. 'Didn't you sometimes long for the company of people other than your brothers?' she asked quietly.

How little she understood! Isolation had been part and parcel of his heritage—even *with* his brothers. Being born the Crown Prince had made his life different from Guido's and Nico's. Even as a boy he had been taken aside by his father—gradually introduced to the mighty task of what lay ahead of him.

'Oh, there was plenty of other company,' he said easily. 'We had friends who came to play with us when we were tiny, and then to learn to ride and swim with us.' But the friends had been cherry-picked—the offspring of Mardivino's aristocracy. The only times he had ever come into contact with the ordinary people of the island were when he had accompanied his father to hand out prizes, or to open a new school or library.

Millie hesitated. She wanted to know this man who was now her husband—to *really* know him. And she didn't just want the answers to her questions, she wanted him to learn to confide in her. She had gone to the trouble of reading a book about Mardivino during their engagement—but the facts were just words on a page, with no real root in reality. It had all happened years and years before she had been born. She wanted to ask Gianferro a very obvious question about his childhood. Almost to get it out of the way— in case it hovered, ever-present, like a great dark cloud in the background.

'It must have been…' She struggled for the right word, but no word could convey the proper sympathy she felt. 'Terrible. When your mother died.'

He hoped that the candlelight concealed the faint frown which creased his brow. Was she now going to probe? To dig at the wound caused by his mother's death? The scar was old now, but it was deep. He had buried his grief as a way of coping at the time, and he had never resurrected it.

'In that I was no different from any other child who loses their mother,' he said flatly. 'Being a prince does not protect you from pain.'

But being a prince meant that you could not show it. She suddenly understood that as clearly as if he had told her.

Millie reached her hand out to lay it on top of his. Her skin was very pale in comparison to the rich olive

of his, and her wedding band was shiny bright as her
fingers curved around his possessively.

But at that moment there was a knock on the door,
and Gianferro couldn't help experiencing a brief moment of relief as he withdrew his hand, welcoming
this interruption to her intrusive line of questioning.
Then his brows creased together in a dark frown.

'Who is this, when I told them to leave us alone?'
he said, almost in an undertone. His frown grew
deeper. 'Come!' he ordered, his voice stern.

It was Alesso who stood there, and Millie's heart
sank. Couldn't he even leave them in peace on their
honeymoon? But on closer inspection she saw that
the handsome Italian's face was tight with tension—
an unbearable, weighty tension.

And there were no words of remonstrance from
Gianferro, for he sprang immediately to his feet, his
face growing pale beneath the olive skin.

'Qu'est-ce que c'est?' he demanded.

Something told her that this was uncharacteristic
behaviour, and Millie stared at him in confusion.

But it was only when Alesso bit his lip and began
to speak that the grim reality of what had happened
began to dawn on her.

'The King is dead!'

Alesso's words were rocks that smote him like an
iron fist, and Gianferro waited for a moment which
seemed to go on for a lifetime. A moment for which
he had spent a lifetime preparing.

'Long live the King!'

And then Alesso dropped deeply to his knees in front of Gianferro and kissed his hand, not raising his head again until Gianferro lightly touched him on the shoulder. It was in that one single instant that the new King realised how much had changed...a lifelong friend would not be—nor could ever be—the same towards him again.

In a heartbeat, everything was different.

An Important Message
from the Editors

Dear Reader,

If you'd enjoy reading romance novels with larger print that's easier on your eyes, let us send you *TWO FREE HARLEQUIN INTRIGUE® NOVELS* in our *NEW LARGER-PRINT EDITION*. These books are complete and unabridged, but the type is set about 25% bigger to make it easier to read. Look inside for an actual-size sample.

By the way, you'll also get a surprise gift with your two free books!

Pam Powers

Peel off Seal and
Place Inside...

LARGER-PRINT
FREE BOOKS
EDITION

THE RIGHT WOMAN

she'd thought she was fine. It took Daniel's words and Brooke's question to make her realize she was far from a full recovery.

She'd made a start with her sister's help and she intended to go forward now. Sarah felt as if she'd been living in a darkened room and some-one had suddenly opened a door, letting in the fresh air and sunshine. She could feel its warmth slowly seeping into the coldest part of her. The feeling was liberating. She realized it was only a small step and she had a long way to go, but she was ready to face life again with Serena and her family behind her.

All too soon, they were saying goodbye and Sarah experienced a moment of sadness for all the years she and Serena had missed. But they had each other now and that's what

She held

PRINTED IN THE U.S.A.
Publisher acknowledges the copyright holder of the excerpt from this individual work as follows:
THE RIGHT WOMAN Copyright © 2004 by Linda Warren. All rights reserved.
® and TM are trademarks owned and used by the trademark owner and/or its licensee

The Harlequin Reader Service™ — Here's How It Works:

Accepting your 2 free Harlequin Intrigue® larger-print books and gift places you under no obligation to buy anything. You may keep the books and gift and return the shipping statement marked "cancel." If you do not cancel, about a month later we'll send you 6 additional Harlequin Intrigue larger-print books and bill you just $4.49 each in the U.S., or $5.24 each in Canada, plus 25¢ shipping & handling per book and applicable taxes if any.* That's the complete price and — compared to cover prices of $5.24 each in the U.S. and $6.24 each in Canada — it's quite a bargain! You may cancel at any time, but if you choose to continue, every month we'll send you 6 more books, which you may either purchase at the discount price or return to us and cancel your subscription.

*Terms and prices subject to change without notice. Sales tax applicable in N.Y. Canadian residents will be charged applicable provincial taxes and GST.

CHAPTER SEVEN

MILLIE felt as if someone had just picked her up and thrown her into a wind tunnel which led to a place of mystery.

Alesso bowed before her, lifted her hand and pressed her fingers to his lips.

'My Queen,' he said brokenly, and Millie sat motionless, as if turned to stone, looking at Gianferro in desperation. How on earth did she respond? But she might as well have been the shadow cast by one of the candles for all the notice he took of her. It wasn't just that he didn't seem to see her—it was almost as though she wasn't there. She felt invisible.

But she pushed her feelings of bewilderment aside and tried to put herself in Gianferro's place. She must not expect guidance nor trouble him for it, certainly not right now. His father had just died, and he had inherited the Kingdom. The role for which he had been preparing all his life was finally his.

She looked into his face. It was hard and cold, and something about the new bleakness in his eyes almost frightened her. What on earth did she *do*?

She was no stranger to bereavement—her own father had died five years ago, and although they had not been close, Millie still remembered the sensation of having had something fundamental torn away from her. And Gianferro had lost his mother, too. To be an orphan was profoundly affecting, even if it happened when you were an adult yourself.

But Millie was now his wife, his help and his emotional support, and she must reach out to him.

She moved over to him and lifted her hand to touch the rigid mask of his face.

'Gianferro,' she whispered. 'I am so sorry. So very, very sorry.'

His eyes flickered towards her, her words startling him out of his sombre reverie. He hoped to God that she wasn't about to start crying. It was not her place to cry—she had barely known the King, and it was important for her to recognise that her role now was to lead. That the people would be looking to her for guidance and she must not crumble or fail.

'Thank you,' he clipped out. 'But the important thing is for the King's work to continue. He has had a long and productive life. There will be sorrow, yes, but we must also celebrate his achievements.' He nodded his head formally. 'You must be a figurehead of comfort to your people,' he said softly.

But not to you, thought Millie, as a great pang wrenched at her heart. Not to you.

'And now we must go back to Solajoya,' he said flatly, and Millie nodded like some obedient, mute servant.

After that everything seemed to happen with an alarming and blurred speed, and with the kind of efficiency which made her think it must have been planned. But of course it would have been. There were always provisions in place to deal with the death of a monarch, even if that monarch were young—and Gianferro's father had been very old indeed.

It was Alesso, not Gianferro, who instructed Millie to wear black, for the new King was busy talking on the phone. Normally, a bride would not have taken black clothes with her on honeymoon, but the instructions she had been given prior to the wedding all made sense now. Gianferro had told her that Royals always travelled with mourning clothes and so she had duly packed some, never thinking in a million years that she might actually need to wear them.

The car ride back to Solajoya was fast and urgent, only slowing down to an almost walking pace when they reached the outskirts of the capital. And Millie had to stifle a gasp—for it was like a city transformed from the one she remembered.

All the flowers and flags and the air of joy which had resonated in the air after their wedding had disappeared. Everything seemed so sombre...so *sad*. People were openly weeping and the buildings were draped in black.

A line of pale-faced dignitaries was awaiting them as they swept into the Palace forecourt, and Gianferro turned to her as the car came to a halt. He had been preoccupied and silent during the journey. She had longed to say something which would comfort him, but she had not been able to find the words—and something inside her had told her that he would not wish to hear them even if she could. She sensed that he was glad to have his position and authority to hide behind. Perhaps for Gianferro it was lucky that expressed emotions would be inappropriate right now.

She reached out a tentative hand towards his, but he didn't even seem to notice, and so she let it fall back onto her lap and stared out of the window instead, her mind muddled and troubled. Her future as Princess had been daunting enough, but as Queen? It didn't bear thinking about.

His voice was low and flat. 'After we have been greeted you will go to our suite,' he instructed. 'I will come to you as soon as I can.'

'When?' she whispered.

'Millie, I do not know. You must be patient.'

And that was that. In a daze, Millie followed behind him as dignitary after dignitary bowed—first to him and then to her.

Once in the suite, she pulled the black hat from her head and looked around the unfamiliar surroundings with a sense of panic.

Now what did she do? She felt as though she had been marooned on a luxurious but inaccessible island, with no one to talk to or confide in. No one to weep with—except that she felt bad about that, too, because there were no tears to shed. She felt sad, yes—but she had only met Gianferro's father once. She hadn't known him at all—and wouldn't it be hypocritical to try to conjure up tears simply because it was expected of her?

Her two sisters-in-law called on her, both dropping deep curtseys before her.

'Please don't feel you have to do that,' begged Millie.

'But we do,' said the taller of them, in a clipped, matter-of-fact voice which was distorted with grief. 'It is simply courtesy, Your Majesty.'

Millie heard the term of address with a sense of mounting disbelief. She had not yet had a chance to get used to it, and it seemed so strange to hear it coming from the lips of two women who were, in effect, her peers.

Ella and Lucy were both English, and both genuinely upset at the King's death. Millie felt like a fraud as she watched Lucy's face crumple with sorrow.

'I feel so bad for Guido!' Lucy wailed. 'He's beating himself up about having stayed away from Mardivino for so many years!'

'Nico's doing exactly the same,' said Ella gloomily. 'He says that if he hadn't given his father so much worry about his dangerous sports over the years, then he might still be alive.'

'But the King was an old man,' said Millie softly. 'And he had been sick for a long time.'

They both stared at her.

'But their mother died when they were little,' said Lucy, swallowing down a gulp. 'And the King was all they had.'

Millie could have kicked herself. She had been trying to offer comfort, that was all—and now she had probably come across as cold and uncaring. Or—even worse—perhaps they thought she was rejoicing in her new role.

She could see the curiosity in their eyes as they looked at her—and was aware that her lofty new status had put distance between them without her ever having had a chance to get to know them properly.

She drew a deep breath. She didn't want them to think her heartless. Or snooty.

'I'm so very sorry,' she said, though she wasn't sure what she was sorry about. Her inability to cry? The distance she was afraid she might have created between herself and the two women who were in the perfect position to be her friends? Or the fact that maybe she should accept that no one would be able to get close to her now that she was Queen?

The funeral took place in the Cathedral where she had been so recently married—but whereas that day had been Technicolored and jubilant, this day was mournful and monochrome.

Millie was exhausted by the time the last of the world leaders had left, and she could see the strain etched deeply on Gianferro's face—he looked as if he had aged by five years. She had sat next to him during the service, but since then she hadn't been able to get close to him. It seemed that everyone wanted a piece of him, and she was the last in line.

Eventually she went to their suite, stripped off her black suit and hat, and soaked for ages in a bath. But he didn't return. She surveyed the froth of exquisite handmade silk negligees which had made up her trousseau, and pushed the drawer shut on them. It seemed somehow wrong to dress in pale and provocative finery when the Palace was officially in mourning.

The honeymoon was over almost before it had begun.

She must have fallen asleep, for she was woken by the sound of a light footfall in the room. She blinked open her eyes and, once they were accustomed to the dim light, saw the silhouetted figure of her husband standing by the bed.

'Gianferro?'

'Who else?' His voice sounded raw, as if someone had been grating at it with a metal implement.

'What time is it?'

'Late. Go back to sleep, Millie.'

But she didn't want to go back to sleep. She had been pushed away by protocol, but there was no protocol here now—not in the dim, darkened privacy of their bedroom.

She lay there, not knowing what to do.

Gianferro wriggled his shoulders to try and remove some of the tension which was making his neck ache. He had been on some kind of autopilot all day. It had been crazy since he, like so many of the courtiers, had been expected to know exactly what to do. But

how could he? Some of the older dignitaries remembered the death of his mother—but he had been only
a child.

Yet the day had gone smoothly—even well. There
had been no hitches or glitches, no assassination
threats or attempts. The massed choirs had inspired
people to say that it had been a beautiful service. And
now his father was buried deep in the ground and he
felt…what?

He didn't know.

Empty, he guessed. As if he had been scrubbed
clean of all emotion. There had been no place for
private grief—not today. Not with the eyes of the
world's press trained like hawks upon him—greedy
for a slip in composure which would be taken as a
sign of weakness and an inability to rule.

'Gianferro?'

Her voice stirred over his shattered senses like a
gentle breeze, but he needed to be alone with his
thoughts. *Wanted* to be alone with them, as he had
been all his life. To sort and sift them and then push
them away. Of all the times to find himself with a
wife there could not possibly have been a worse one.
'Go to sleep,' he said tightly.

But Millie had had days of being pushed away. No,
she would not go to sleep! She sat bolt upright in bed
and switched on the light. She heard him suck in a
ragged breath. Was he shocked that she was naked?
Was it also a sign of mourning for the Monarch that

she should be swathed in some concealing night attire?

He had taken most of his uniform off, and was standing there in just a pair of dark tapered trousers and a crisp white shirt which he had undone at the collar. He looked as if he had stepped straight out of one of the many portraits which lined the corridors of the Palace. A man from another age. But maybe that wasn't so fanciful—for weren't Kings ageless and timeless?

The King is dead…long live the King.

'Gianferro?' she whispered, more timidly now.

How could it be that when his senses felt dead— his feelings as barren as some desert landscape—desire should leap up like some hot and pulsing and irresistible hidden well?

'Millie,' he said simply.

It was the most human and approachable she had ever heard him, and that one word stirred in her a response which was purely instinctive. She held her arms open to him. 'Come here.'

She looked so clean and fresh and pure. So wholesome—glowing like some luminescent candle in the soft light which bathed her.

So he went to her, allowed her to tightly enfold him in her arms, and she smoothed at his head with soothing and rhythmical fingers, and he felt some of the unbearable tension leave him.

Millie felt as though she was poised on a knife-edge—one wrong move and he would retreat from her once more. And yet it was not sex she sought, but comfort she wanted to *give* to him—for at this moment he was not King. Just a man who had lost his only surviving parent and who must now take up the heavy burden of leadership.

Time lost all meaning as she cradled him the way she supposed women had cradled their men since time began. And again, relying solely on an instinct which seemed to spring bone-deep from some hidden and unknown source, she began to massage the tight knot of his shoulders.

'That's...that's good,' he said thickly.

She carried on, working at the hard muscle as if her life depended on it. And when she moved her hands to unbutton the rest of his shirt he made no attempt to stop her, just remained exactly where he was—his head still resting on her shoulder as if it was too heavy for him to lift.

She slid the stiff, starched garment from his shoulders, exposing the silken olive skin which sheathed the hard musculature of his lean body. And then she bent her head and kissed him very softly on the cheek, and a pent-up sigh escaped him.

He did lift his head then, and he looked at her—at her eyes, which were innocent and troubled and yet hungry, too. And something inside him erupted into life—something strong and dark and powerful and unrecognisable. He moved his arms around her back, crushed her breasts against his bare chest and kissed her—a kiss which was fierce and all-consuming.

Beneath the heady, hard pressure of that kiss Millie went under as if she was drowning. She wanted to tell him that it was comfort she was offering him, that they didn't have to do this—but he did not seem to want her words. And wasn't she secretly glad that she did not have to say them?

He tore himself away and stripped off his trousers, and he was so aroused that for a moment she felt a tremor of fear as she looked at him. But he vanquished that fear with the expert touch of his hands and replaced it with desire, stroking her until she was molten and aching.

He moved above her, his big, hard body blotting out the light. His face was shadowed, but she didn't care. Nothing mattered other than the primitive longing to have him close to her again, to have him inside her, to feel the sense of triumph when he shuddered helplessly in her arms.

She moved distractedly and caught him by the shoulders.

'Sì,' he murmured, as if in answer to an unspoken question. When he thrust into her she cried out, and he stopped, frowning down at her. 'I am hurting you?'

Would it sound pathetic to tell him that the sensation had overwhelmed her—both mentally and physically? That he filled her so deeply that he seemed to have pierced her very heart? Or that making love at this time of loss seemed to take on such a poignant sense of significance?

But Gianferro did not like analysis at the best of

times, and right now would be the worst of times to try to tell him. She shook her head. 'N-no. No, you're not hurting me.'

But he held back a little as he began to move again, and never had he found it so difficult to contain himself. He was a most accomplished lover, and yet now he wanted to pump his seed into her without restraint. Yet he could not, for he was also a generous lover. Instead he switched off, and concentrated solely on her pleasure—using the vast wealth of experience he had learned from so many women over the years.

Millie felt torn in two. Her body couldn't help but respond to what he was doing to her, but his face was the dark and beautiful face of a stranger. He looked so intent...so focused. There was no love nor tenderness nor emotion on those carved features.

But you can't have everything, Millie, her greedy body seemed to cry out to her, and then feeling took over completely and she was lost. Lost...

He saw her face dissolve into passionate release and at last he let go. It seemed as if he had been waiting all his life for this to happen. He had always been a silent lover, but now he called out—a faltering, broken cry—for it was as if he had been locked in tight bands of iron and someone had suddenly snapped them open.

The power of his orgasm seized him like a mighty wave, caught him unawares, despite the fact that he had longed for its incomparable release. It threw him into a maelstrom of sensation so intense that he gasped aloud as wave upon wave of pleasure made him wonder if he could stay conscious. For a moment he felt weak with it—this alien and unwelcome realisation that he could be lured and weakened like any other man.

He shut his eyes for a second, and when he opened them again it was to stare up at dancing diamonds of light reflected from the waterfall of the chandelier. How elusively simple life could be at times. He expelled a long, sighing breath. If only...

Millie heard him and propped herself up on her elbow, with her hair falling all over the place, flushed with pleasure and aware of the first shimmerings of sexual confidence. He had wanted to sleep and she had persuaded him not to! In his time of grief and distress she had brought him solace in the only way she knew how.

'Gianferro?'

Her voice was like an intruder and his eyes became shuttered. When before had his steely will been bent? And why now—by her? Was it her unworldliness which had struck a chord in him—or the fact that death made you want to grab onto the life-force and embrace it, hang onto it as if you needed to be convinced in the most fundamental way of all that you were still so very much alive yourself?

But this would not do. There was much to be done and he must not be distracted. Furthermore, Millie must learn that he would *not* be distracted. She must bend to *his* will—not expect him to bend to *hers*. It was the only way.

'Gianferro?' she repeated, hating herself for the diffident note which had crept into her voice.

'Go to sleep, Millie,' he said, and shut his eyes again.

She had been hoping for kisses. She was not asking for words of love that he did not feel for her—just for the intimacy and closeness of being sleepy together. What had just taken place had shaken her to the core, and while she was still very new to all this, she was not stupid—it had shaken Gianferro, too, she knew it had. And yet despite the wonder and the strength of what had just happened he lay there now as if his body had been carved from stone—as distant as one of the rocks out at sea. When this moment—surely—was one when they could be as close as two people could be.

She turned onto her back and lay looking up at the ceiling, feeling suddenly very alone. Was this what her marriage was going to be like? And if so, could she bear it?

He had corrected her when she had asked if being Royal meant being remote, implying that she had misunderstood him—that he had meant to say removed.

But she didn't believe him. For at this precise moment he was as remote as it was possible for any man to be.

She listened to the deepening of his breathing and realised he had fallen asleep.

Millie bit her lip.

For sanity's sake—she wasn't going to think about it.

CHAPTER EIGHT

MILLIE drew a deep breath. 'Gianferro?'

The King looked up from his desk, his mind clearing as he saw his wife hovering in the doorway of his study. How beautiful she looked today—with her pale hair wound into some complicated confection which lay at the back of her long, slender neck. She wore a simple blue dress, which emphasised her lithe and athletic build and her long legs. Legs which had last night been bare and wrapped around his naked back. He smiled with satisfaction. 'What is it, *cara mia*?'

'Do you have a moment?' she questioned.

The faintest glimmer of a frown creased his brow. Millie, as much as anyone, knew just how tight his schedule was. 'What's on your mind?'

She wondered what he would say if she told him the truth—that she was feeling lonely and isolated, and that a night-time dose of passion did not compensate for those feelings. But she could not tell him. Gianferro was far too busy to be worrying about *her* problems—which to an outsider would probably not look like problems at all. And why would they?

To an observer, she had everything. A gorgeous husband who made love to her with such sweet abandon that sometimes she seriously thought that her body could not withstand such pleasure. She lived in a Palace and she could have whatever she pleased. The things which other women dreamed of were hers for the taking…even if, ironically, they were not what she coveted.

'I want you to cover your exquisite body in jewels,' Gianferro had murmured to her huskily in bed one night.

'But I'm not into jewels!' Millie had protested.

'No?' Lazily he had drifted a fingertip from neck to cleavage, and she had shivered with anticipation. 'Then I shall have to be ''into'' them for you, shan't I, Millie?' His black eyes had glittered. 'I shall buy you a sapphire as big as a pigeon's egg, and it will echo your eyes and hang just above your glorious breasts and remind me of how I bury my mouth in them and suckle on their sweetness.'

When the man you loved said something like that what woman *wouldn't* be putty in his hands? Suddenly the idea of a priceless necklace *did* appeal—but only because Gianferro would choose it. For her and only her. As if it meant something— *really* meant something—instead of just being a symbol of possession. An expensive bauble for his wife. A material reward for her devotion to duty as his Queen because he was unable to give her what she really craved—for him to love her. Properly. The way that she loved him.

And she did.

How could she fail to love the man who had awoken the woman in her in every way that counted and set her free? She had been living in a two-dimensional world before Gianferro had stormed in with such vibrant and pulsating life.

He had taken her and transformed her—moulded her into his Queen and his wife. At least externally he had. Inside she was aware of her own vulnerability—of a great, aching realisation that he would never return the love she felt for him.

Sometimes she looked at him in bed at night, when he was sleeping, and could scarcely believe that he was hers. Well, in so much as someone like Gianferro could be anyone's.

He was everything a man should and could be—strong and proud and intelligent, with a sensuality which seemed to shimmer off him. The leader of the pack—and weren't all women programmed to desire the undisputed leader? Especially as he treated her like…well, like a princess, she supposed. Except that she wasn't. Not any more. She was now the Queen.

The Coronation had been terrifying—the glittering crown which had been placed on her head at the solemn moment had seemed almost as heavy as she was. But at least she had been expecting it—had been warned about the weight of it—and Alesso had suggested she practise walking around the apartments with it on her head.

'It takes a little getting used to—the wearing of a crown, Your Serene Majesty.'

It had seemed more than a little bizarre to be wearing jeans and a T-shirt and a priceless heirloom on her head! Millie's eyes had widened. 'It weighs a *ton*!' she'd exclaimed, as she had lowered it onto her blonde hair.

'Do not tilt your head so. Yes, that is better. Now, practise sitting down on the throne, Your Majesty,' he had instructed, and Millie had falteringly obeyed, feeling like one of those women who had to carry their crops home on top of their heads!

At least she hadn't let anyone down on the big day—herself included. The newspapers had praised the 'refreshing innocence' of the new young Queen, and Millie had stared unblinkingly at the photographs.

Was that really her?

To Millie herself she seemed to resemble a startled young deer which had just heard a gunshot deep in the forest. Her eyes looked huge and her mouth unsmiling. But then she had been coached in that, too. It was a solemn occasion—heralded by the death of the old King—not a laughing matter.

Afterwards, of course, there had been celebrations in the Palace, and Millie had overheard Lulu exclaiming, 'I can't believe I'm sister to a *queen*!' and had seen Gianferro's brief and disapproving frown.

At least that had dissolved away the last of her residual doubts about Lulu. She could see now that her sister would not have made a good consort to Gianferro—she was far too independent.

And me? What about me? Millie had caught a reflection of herself in one of the silvered mirrors which lined the Throne Room. *I am directionless and without a past, and therefore I am the perfect wife for him.* The image thrown back at her was a sylph-like figure clad in pure and flowing white satin. In a way, she looked more of a bride on her Coronation day than when she had married—but she had learnt more than one lesson since then, and had toned down her make-up to barely anything.

Yes, her husband revered and respected her, and made love to her, but he was not given to words of love. Not once had he said *I love you*—not in any language. And Millie was beginning to suspect that was because he simply did not have the capacity for the fairytale kind of love that every woman secretly dreamed of. How could he?

He had been rigidly schooled for the isolating rigours of kingship, and his mother had been torn away from him at such a crucial stage in his development. A mother might have softened the steeliness which lay at the very core of his character—shown him that to love was not a sign of weakness.

Millie had tried from time to time to talk to him on a more intimate level, but she had seen his eyes narrow before he smoothly changed the subject. *Don't even go there,* his body language seemed to say. And so she didn't. Because what choice did she have?

Only in bed, when his appetite was sated—in that brief period of floating in sensation alone before reality snapped back in—did he ever let his guard

down, and then it was only fractionally. Then he
would touch his lips to her hair almost indulgently,
and this would lull her into a sense of expectation
which would invariably be smashed.

She wanted him to tell her about his day—to confide in her what his thoughts had been—just as if they
were any normal newly-wed couple, but it was like
drawing blood from a stone. They *weren't* a normal
couple, nor ever would be. And he didn't seem to
even want to try to be.

Gianferro was looking at her now, as she hovered
uncertainly in the door of his study. It was a gaze
laced with affection, it had to be said, but also with
slight impatience—for his time was precious and she
must never forget that.

'Yes, Millie?'

She laced her fingers together. 'You remember on
our honeymoon I said that I wanted to learn French?'

'Yes. Yes.' He nodded impatiently.

'Well, I've changed my mind.' She could see his
small smile of satisfaction. 'I think it should be
Italian.'

'Really?' he questioned coolly.

'Well, yes. Italian is your first language.'

'I am fluent in four,' he said, with a touch of arrogance.

'It's your language of choice.' She looked at him.
'In bed,' she added boldly.

His eyes narrowed for just a second before his
smile became dismissive. He loved her eagerness and

her joy in sex—but did she really imagine that she could come in here at will and tempt him away from affairs of state? Very deliberately he put his pen down in a gesture of closing the subject. 'Very well. I shall speak to Alesso about selecting you a tutor.'

But something in the cold finality of his eyes made Millie rebel. She tried to imagine herself in one of the luxurious rooms of the Palace, with the finest tutor that money and privilege could provide, and realised it was just going to be more of the same. Isolation. 'But, if you recall, I said that I would like to learn in a class with other people.'

'And I think that, if *you* recall, I hinted that such a scenario would be inappropriate.' His eyes narrowed. 'What is wrong with taking your lessons here, *cara*?'

Take courage, Millie—he'll never know unless you tell him. 'Sometimes I feel a little…lonely, here at the Palace.' She saw his frown deepen and she hastily amended her words, not wanting him to think that she was spoilt or ungrateful. 'Oh, I know that you're busy—of course you are—but…' Her words tapered off, because she wasn't quite sure where she was going with them.

'You are still not with child?'

Millie stared at him and the nagging little feeling of guilt she had been doing her best to quash reared its mocking head. Perhaps a baby *was* the answer. Maybe she should throw her Pills away and no one would ever be the wiser. 'N-no.'

'You wish to consult the Palace obstetrician?'

There was something so chillingly matter-of-fact about his question that hot on the heels of her wavering came rebellion, and Millie bristled. As if a baby would solve everything! As if she was little more than a brood mare! 'I think it's early days yet, don't you?' she questioned, trying to keep her voice reasonable. 'We've only been married for six months.'

He quelled the oddly painful feeling of disappointment. She was right—it was early days indeed. Here was one thing he could *not* command. An heir would be his just as soon as nature—and fate—decreed it.

'Yes, that is so,' he agreed, and gave her a soft smile. 'What about your horses?' he questioned, for he had acquired for her two of the finest Andalusian mares that money could buy. 'Surely they provide adequate amusement for you?'

Millie bristled even more. 'It may have escaped your notice, but horses do not speak.'

'Yet the grooms tell me that you communicate with them almost as if they *could* speak.' His voice dipped with pride. 'That your enthusiasm for all things equine equals the energy you put in to your charity work.'

She knew that in his subtle way he was praising her—telling her that she made a good Queen and that there was plenty to occupy her without her trying to make a life for herself outside the rigid confines of the Palace. She could see that from *his* point of view it would be so much easier for a tutor to be brought in.

'And your English sisters-in-law,' he continued. 'You like Ella and Lucy, do you not?'

'Yes, I like them very much,' said Millie truthfully. But Ella and Lucy were different, and not just because they were mothers. Their relationships with their husbands were close and inclusive—and that wasn't just her imagining. She had seen them sometimes, at State Banquets, behaving with all the decorum expected of their position—but occasionally sneaking a small, shared look or a secret smile. Gianferro never did that with her.

She knew that comparisons were wrong, and could lead you nowhere except to dissatisfaction, and Millie wanted to be contented with her lot—or rather she wanted to make the best of what she had, not yearn for something which could never be hers.

But sometimes it was hard not to—especially when her sisters-in-law had genuine love-matches. Theirs had not been marriages of convenience, where the winning hand had been the bride-to-be's innocence and inexperience.

'I guess I don't really know them that well,' she said thoughtfully.

'Well, then?' said Gianferro impatiently. 'Invite them round for tea! Get to know them a little better!'

His arrogance and condescension took her breath away and strengthened her determination to fight for a little freedom.

'Very well, I will—but I should still like to go to a class,' she said quietly. 'What harm can it do?'

Gianferro drummed his fingers on the polished rosewood of his desk. He was not used to having his wishes thwarted, but he recognised a new light of purpose in his wife's eyes. 'It could...complicate things,' he murmured.

'How?'

Would she believe him if he told her? Or was this going to be one of the lessons she needed to learn for herself? He knew what she was trying to do—trying to dip into a 'normal' life once more—but she could not. Her life had changed in ways she had not even begun to comprehend. He felt a fleeting wave of regret that it should be so, which was swiftly followed by irritation that she would not be guided by his experience.

'It will not be as you imagine it to be,' he warned. 'Being Royal sets you apart.'

'I think I'd prefer to find that out for myself,' said Millie, but a smile was twitching at her lips, because suddenly this one small blow for freedom felt important. Tremendously important.

'Very well,' he said shortly. 'I will speak to Alesso.'

It was clear from his attitude that the usually sanguine Alesso disapproved of her request almost as much as Gianferro did, but Millie held firm and two weeks later she was allowed to go to an Italian class, accompanied by a bodyguard.

The class had been chosen by Alesso, and was held in a large room at the British Embassy. Millie was greeted by the Ambassador's wife, who dropped a deep curtsey before her. She wanted to say *Please don't make a fuss*, except that she knew her words would be redundant. People *did* make a fuss—indeed, they would be disappointed if they were not allowed to! But she had given Alesso prior warning that her participation in the class was not to be announced.

'I'd like to just slip in unnoticed,' said Millie softly. She had dressed as anonymously as possible—a knee-length skirt and a simple sweater, for while the Mardivinian winter was mild, there was a faint chill to the air.

Alesso had raised his eyebrows. 'Certainly, Your Majesty.'

She smiled. 'Loosen up,' she said softly. 'It's only an Italian class!'

The tutor had his back to her when she walked in—he was busy scrawling verbs on a blackboard—and as the door opened he turned round and frowned, pushing back the dark, shoulder-length hair which hung almost to his shoulders.

'You are late!' he admonished.

Clearly he didn't recognise her! Millie bit back a smile as she heard the slight inrush of breath from the Ambassador's wife, and almost imperceptibly shook her head in a silent *don't fuss* command. 'Sorry,' she said meekly, quickly making her way to a spare place at the back of the room. 'I'll just sit quietly and try to catch up.'

He nodded. 'Make sure you do.'

The next hour was spent busily trying to retain fact after fact and word after word. For a brief moment Millie realised how long it was since she had actually used her brain—not since school, and then not as much as she could have done.

But she found that she was enjoying herself, and soon lost herself in the challenge of learning something for the first time.

Her first faltering attempts at speaking aloud were greeted with smiles from the others, but she found herself smiling when *their* turn came. They were all in the same boat, and the sense of belonging she experienced filled her with a warm glow.

At the end of the class the others began to file out, and Millie was just gathering her books together when the tutor strolled down towards her and paused by her desk. He looked more like an artist than a teacher, she thought, with his long dark hair and jeans and T-shirt.

'You enjoyed my class?' he questioned.

Millie nodded. 'Very much. You made it seem… easy!'

'Ah! You should not say such things.' He laughed. 'Or the expectation for you to become my star pupil will be too high!'

'Okay, you made it seem really difficult!'

He was frowning now. It was not a frown of displeasure, but as if he was trying to place her, and Millie's heart sank.

'Don't I know you, *signora*?' he questioned softly.

'I don't think we've met.' Millie began to shuffle her books in order to put an end to a line of questioning which struck her as extremely inappropriate, but it seemed he was not to be deterred.

'Your face is…familiar.'

She guessed she couldn't have it both ways—she couldn't pull rank if she was trying to keep her identity secret! It was true that as she had been sitting at the back of the class only the tutor would have seen her face—but she couldn't do that week in, week out. And when she stopped to think about it hadn't she been living in cloud-cuckoo land even thinking that she could—with a dirty great bodyguard stationed outside the door?

'Is it?'

He gave a low laugh. 'You are the image of our new Queen!'

Millie sighed. 'That's because I am.'

'You are joking me?'

Millie laughed as his English deserted him in his confusion. 'Okay, I am!'

He gave a long, low whistle. 'I have the Queen in my class?' he questioned incredulously. 'The Queen of Mardivino?'

Millie smiled. 'Is that a problem for you?'

'For me, no! But perhaps for you?'

'I don't see why.' She allowed herself to believe the illusion and it was both heady and seductive.

His eyes narrowed. 'Why are you not being taught within the Palace?'

'Perhaps I want to experience life outside it,' she answered slowly.

'The caged bird?' he questioned thoughtfully. 'Who longs to break free?'

'You're being very impertinent!' she remonstrated.

'Am I?' He stared at her. 'You say you wish to experience life—and life outside the Palace means that people say what is on their minds.' He hesitated. 'What must I call you?'

She gave it only a split-second's thought. In this— if only in this—she would be like everyone else. 'My name is Millie,' she said firmly. 'You must call me Millie.'

'And I am Oliviero.' He smiled then, a genuine smile which made his eyes crinkle. 'Your secret is safe with me...Millie—though I doubt that it will remain so. But I can and will tell you this—while in my class, you are simply another pupil, and the others will respect that or they will be...' He shrugged and clicked his fingers in a dismissive gesture.

'Turfed out?' supplied Millie helpfully.

'Turfed out? Yes, it is just that!' His smile grew wider. 'I sometimes forget that it is the teacher who also learns!'

And Millie smiled back.

The challenge of studying added an extra dimension to her life, and she threw herself into her work with a new-found enthusiasm which was very gratifying.

She wasn't naïve enough to suppose that the rest of the class remained oblivious to her true identity, for their manner towards her was subtly deferential. But no one bothered her, or questioned her, or was intrusive.

She was always the last to leave—mainly to avoid being seen with her bodyguard, but also because she had grown to enjoy her little chats with Oliviero. He alone, of all people, treated her just as Millie. With him she felt like the person she knew she really was, deep inside. Not the Queen—a person who always led the conversation and was listened to with deference—but someone with whom she could have a genuine laugh. A small thing, but a precious and cherished one, and it reminded her of a very different life indeed.

Millie hadn't realised quite how much freedom she would lose when she married her Prince, but in a tiny way this compensated.

Her false paradise lasted for precisely one month, until the morning when Alesso knocked at the door of her sitting room. She had been sitting looking at an Italian newspaper. Oliviero had told her that she would understand almost none of it—and he had been right!—but that the best way to become fluent with a language was to familiarise yourself with it as much as possible. Each word she correctly identified felt as though she had found a nugget of gold!

'Come!' she called, and saw the tall, dark figure of Alesso, his face unsmiling. 'Oh, hello, Alesso!' she said brightly.

'Majesty.' He gave a deep bow.

'I'm just finishing up here.' She glanced at her watch, wondering what had prompted this rare and unheralded visit. 'I don't have to be at the Women's Refuge for another hour, do I?'

'The King wishes to speak with you.'

It was pointless to say, *Couldn't the King have come and told me that himself?* Because that wasn't how it worked. Millie rose to her feet. 'Very well. He is at work?'

'He awaits you in your suite, Majesty.'

'At this time of day?' she asked in surprise. But it was a rhetorical question and Alesso said nothing. Even if he had known the answer he would still have said nothing, for his first loyalty lay towards Gianferro. As did everyone else's.

Still unsmiling and unspeaking, Alesso accompanied her through the long portrait-lined corridors towards their suite of rooms, and Millie began to feel unaccountably nervous. 'I do know the way!' she joked.

'I gave His Majesty assurance that I would conduct you there myself,' he said formally.

The unwelcome thought flitted into her mind that it was like being led towards the gallows. A little knot of unknown fear at the pit of her stomach began to grow into a medium-sized ball, and by the time Alesso knocked and then opened the door her heart was racing.

It raced even harder when she saw Gianferro standing there, his face a study in anger, dark and brooding, and looking like she had never seen him look before.

'*Grazie*, Alesso,' he clipped out.

There was silence as she heard the door being closed behind his aide, and then Gianferro spoke, in a harsh voice she didn't recognise.

'I think you owe me some kind of explanation, don't you, Millie?'

CHAPTER NINE

MILLIE stared at the unfamiliar sight of a Gianferro whose face was contorted by fury. Normally it was implacable. Enigmatic. It wasn't just that he had been brought up to conceal his innermost feelings—Gianferro didn't *do* big emotions. She felt the shivering of apprehension suddenly tiptoeing over her skin as she stared at him.

'Explanation for what?'

The fury became transmuted into a look of icy disdain, and somehow that made her even *more* apprehensive. 'Oh, come, come, Millie,' he said silkily. 'I am not a stupid man.'

'Perhaps not,' she said shakily. 'But you are being a very confusing one right now. How can I give you an "explanation" when I don't have a clue what it is I'm supposed to have done!'

The black eyes narrowed and he regarded her silently, and Millie was reminded of some dark, jungle predator in that infinitesimal moment of stillness before it pounced.

'How is *Oliviero*?' he clipped out.

For a moment she had no idea what he was talking about—and when she did it made even less sense. Millie frowned. 'You mean my Italian teacher?'

'Or your lover?'

She stared at him. 'Are you...*crazy*?' she whispered.

'Maybe a little, but perhaps I am not the only one.' His mouth curved into a cruelly sarcastic smile. 'Does it feed your ego to make some poor little teacher fall in love with you?'

'What are you talking about?' she asked, in genuine confusion. 'Oliviero is not a "poor little" *anything*—he happens to be a brilliant linguist.'

'My, but how you defend him!' he mocked.

Millie felt as though someone had just exploded a bomb in the centre of her world, and she had no idea why. But Gianferro was angry—really, *really* angry—and the first thing she needed to do was to calm him down.

'Won't you tell me what this is all about?' she pleaded.

Gianferro's breathing was ragged, rarely could he remember feeling such an all-consuming rage, and yet her face betrayed nothing other than what seemed like genuine confusion. Unless she was a better actress than he had bargained for.

'Very well.' His dark eyes sparked accusation. 'The editor of the *Mardivino Times* rang Alesso this morning to ask whether anyone would like to comment on the rumours sweeping the capital about my wife.'

'R-rumours?' she stammered, in horror. 'What kind of rumours?'

He heard the faltering of her words with a grim

kind of understanding. Now, that—*that*—sounded like guilt. 'You don't know?'

'Of course I don't know—Gianferro, please tell me!'

He felt the acrid taste of jealousy and rage tainting his mouth with their poison as he glanced down at a piece of paper which was covered with Alesso's handwriting. 'Apparently you have grown *close* to—and I quote—"the devastatingly handsome young Italian who has broken hearts all over Solajoya".' He looked at her trembling lips, cold to their appeal. 'Well?' he shot out. 'What have you to say?'

The accusation was so unjust and so unwarranted that part of her wanted to just tell him to go to hell and storm out of the room. But she couldn't do that—and not just because that wasn't the way queens behaved. She was his wife and this was a genuine misunderstanding.

'It isn't like that at all! He has just been…kind to me.'

His mouth twisted in scorn. 'I'll bet he has.'

'Gianferro, please.' Her voice gentled. 'Stop it.'

But he couldn't stop it, nor did he want to. It was as if he had stepped onto a rollercoaster with no idea of how to get off again. If she had obeyed his orders then she would never have found herself in this position! Black eyes bored into her. 'So you do not deny that you have spent time alone with him after every class?'

'That's one way of looking at it,' she said calmly. 'But that isn't how it—'

He sliced through her words. 'Just you and him? No one else?' If she denied this then he would know that she was lying, for had not her bodyguard been questioned just minutes earlier?

'Well…yes. But nothing has happened—'

'Yet.'

'How dare you?'

'No, Millie,' he said heavily. 'How dare *you*? How dare you be so thoughtless, so *naïve*?'

'I thought that what was one of the reasons you married me!' she retorted. 'I thought you liked that!'

He believed her now, but she must understand that he would not tolerate such behaviour. 'You'd better sit down,' he said heavily.

'I don't want to sit down. And certainly not if I'm going to be treated like a naughty child.'

'Don't you realise how people talk?' he demanded. 'How quickly rumours can gather force in a place like this?'

'And how quickly you believe them!'

'Then prove me wrong!' he challenged.

She had to convince him that she was completely innocent—and, more than that, didn't she owe him some kind of explanation for how this ridiculous misunderstanding had arisen? Shouldn't she try to make him understand why she'd acted the way she had? Dared she admit that Oliviero's attitude had been like a breath of fresh air blowing through the formal world of the Court?

'He made me feel like me,' she admitted slowly.

'Do *not* talk to me in riddles, Millie. Explain.'

'He seemed to like me just as a person. As me— *Millie*. Not because I was Queen.' Her blue eyes were full of appeal. 'He didn't even know for sure who I was. Not at first.'

His eyes were hard. 'Now you really *are* being naïve. Of *course* he knew!

'I didn't tell him.'

'The whole class knew.' He sighed. 'Do you not think that people might not have noticed the Royal crest on the car? The presence of a hulking great bodyguard outside? The fact that you were accompanied to the class by the Ambassador's wife herself? Did you not consider that people might recognise you from your photographs?'

'He may have known,' she said staunchly. 'They may all have known—but it didn't seem to matter. It made no difference to the way they treated me.'

'Oh, you little fool, Millie!' he retorted. 'How do you think I found out all this?'

She stared at him. 'From the bodyguard?'

'No, not from the bodyguard! From the Italian himself!' he snapped. 'Via the newspaper! He has been hawking your story round to the highest bidder!'

'But there is no story!' she protested.

He saw the hurt which clouded her big blue eyes and felt a momentary pang, knowing that he was about to disillusion her further, that this would shatter her trust completely. Could he do it? Had he not taken enough from her already in his quest for the perfect wife?

His mouth hardened. He had to.

'Maybe there isn't,' he agreed. 'But there was enough of a story for the editor to be interested. "A special closeness…"' His eyes narrowed. 'Do you deny there was that?'

'A closeness?' Millie rubbed at her eyes. 'Yes, probably. But special? Yes, probably that, too—if a person makes you feel something that other people can't.'

He flinched, for the barb was directed as much at him as at anyone. 'And what was that?' he asked quietly.

'He made me feel…' Millie shrugged as she struggled to find a word that didn't make her sound pathetic. Or ungrateful. 'Ordinary, I guess.'

'But you are not ordinary, Millie. You never have been and you certainly never will be now.'

It was a bit like having someone tell you that Father Christmas was not real—an unwelcome but necessary step into the world of grown-ups—and Millie recognised that Gianferro was right. She wasn't ordinary— she had bade farewell to the ease of an anonymous life on the day she had taken her wedding vows. She was Queen, and she must act accordingly.

She felt the sting of tears at the back of her eyes. 'I've been so stupid,' she whispered.

Inexplicably, her disillusionment hurt him more than her tears, and he went to her then, pulled her to her feet and gathered her into his arms and into his embrace. She was stiff and as awkward as a puppet, and maybe so was he—just a little—for to comfort a woman was a new experience for him. To touch without sensual intent was like walking on uncharted territory, but he began to stroke her hair and gradually she began to relax.

'Maybe I am the one who should be sorry,' he said softly, and for possibly the first time in his life he tried to see things from someone else's point of view. He frowned. 'You think that I neglect you?'

Was this part of being grown-up too—accepting her role completely—telling him that no, he didn't neglect her? 'You are a very busy man,' she said evasively.

He pushed her away a little, so that he could look down at her face. 'Which does not answer my question.'

'I think it does, Gianferro. There are only so many hours in the day, and yours are filled with work. So many demands on your time—and I don't want to become another burden when already you have so many.'

'Would it help if I made space in my diary once a week—so that we could have dinner alone together no matter what?'

They would never be *completely* alone, of course... there would always be servants and aides hovering in the background. But she recognised that he was making an effort, that the offer itself was an important gesture of trying to see things her way. And in response she must try to see things *his* way.

'That would be lovely,' she said evenly.

His eyes narrowed. He had softened the blow... now came the steel punch which lay behind it. 'You do realise that these lessons will have to stop?' he questioned softly. 'That you cannot be friends with this man any more?'

She nodded, determined not to let him see her hurt or her sinking realisation that in the end Gianferro had got his own way. Maybe he always did. 'Of course I do.' She must show him that she could be strong, that these things did not matter. 'It's just taking me a bit of time to make the adjustment,' she admitted with a smile.

He pulled her closer. 'And that is perfectly natural. Perhaps you are a little homesick? Would it help if I arranged for you to take a trip back to England?'

And be even further away from him?

She wasn't homesick at all. She was lovesick. Wanting to give so much more to him than he wanted, or needed. Wanting time to lie in his arms, to lazily trace her fingertips over the beautiful contours of his face. Wanting him not to be so frazzled with work that he would not fall into an instant sleep once they had made love. They were talking now in a way they rarely did, and it made her feel so close to him that she wanted to hang onto the feeling for ever, to imprint it on her mind.

She wound her arms around his neck and looked up into his face. 'Oh, Gianferro,' she sighed. 'Won't you just kiss me?'

Her parted lips were pure temptation, as was the buttercup tumble of her hair, and Gianferro hesitated only for a fraction of a moment before lowering his head, his lips touching hers in a kiss which was supposed to be fleeting. But then he felt them part, and the warm eagerness of her breath as it heated him. She was always so responsive! As a pupil, she had far surpassed all his expectations.

But the word *pupil* reminded him of her folly, and the brief tang of anger heated his blood, set it pulsing around his veins. His body responded with the age-old antidote to anger. The pressure of his lips hardened and he pulled her body against his almost roughly, feeling her instant response as her soft curves melted into his.

Millie felt the heated clamour of her breasts as they became swollen and hard, and opened her mouth eagerly as his tongue flicked in and out, tightening her grip on the broad shoulders, not daring to touch him anywhere else in case he stopped.

But he didn't stop. He touched her aching breasts, then slid his hand down to mould the contours of her hips, and she could scarcely believe it when it began to ruck up the hem of her dress, his fingertips finding the silken temptation of her inner thigh.

'Gianferro!' she gasped indistinctly against his mouth.

'What is it?' he drawled.

She was so on fire with need that she paid no heed to logic or good sense. To the fact that he had insulted and accused her—only to the knowledge that she wanted him so badly. 'Make love to me,' she said brokenly.

Dimly he was aware that he had about half an hour until his next appointment, and that this was sheer and utter madness—but what other feeling in the world could suck you so willingly down into its dark and erotic vortex and obliterate every other?

He stared down at her, at the pale upturned face and the parted lips, and he sucked in a hot and hungry breath as he forced himself to resist them. 'Do you want me and only me?' he demanded.

'Yes!' she gasped. 'You know I do!'

In one corner of the room was a chaise longue which was rarely used, and he pushed her towards it. She went willingly, unprotesting, not daring to speak in case that broke the spell, brought him to his senses.

For she had never seen Gianferro like this before— so fervent and intent, almost…not out of control, no—for that would be alien to his nature—but like a man who had for once given in to what he truly wanted rather than what was expected of him.

His face dark, his eyes almost unseeing, he pushed her down and slid her panties right off, brazenly touching the moist heat which seared him, a grim, hard smile curving his lips as she writhed in response. And then he unzipped himself and Millie watched him—the hunger of her body momentarily suspended by the unbelievable sight of Gianferro moving towards her—*in broad daylight*—to make love to her.

It all happened very quickly—but she guessed there was time for nothing else. There was no formality, no tenderness and no foreplay—but she didn't need it, and neither did he. God, she had never felt so on fire with need! A small cry of anguished pleasure formed on her lips, but he kissed it away with a hard and efficient kiss which muffled it as he thrust deep inside her.

Maybe it was the sheer incongruity of what they were doing in Gianferro's study in the middle of the day which heightened her senses to an almost unbearable pitch, but her appetite was so sharpened that her orgasm happened almost immediately, and she felt him give one hard, final thrust before he too followed, his dark head falling onto her shoulder.

They stayed like that for a moment—she could feel his breath, warm and rapid against her neck—and then he raised his head, his dark eyes glittering with a look she dared not analyse for fear of what she might read there.

'Does that make you feel better, Millie?' he questioned slowly, as he carefully eased himself out of her.

Her euphoria evaporated. He made it sound as if she had just been given a dose of medicine! But she wouldn't let her hurt show…indeed, wasn't she being a little precious to *feel* hurt? Gianferro had just done something extremely out of character—something they had both needed—and he had done it without a thought to propriety. She must be making some kind of progress, and she should seize on that and cherish it.

She wound her arms around his neck. 'Oh, yes,' she whispered. 'That was wonderful.'

Gianferro's eyes narrowed as he untangled her arms. 'You'd better straighten yourself up.'

Millie's cheeks grew pink as she reached down to find her crumpled panties, aware that she was all sticky and that it was miles back to her own office. 'Can you pass me some tissues?'

Gianferro stared, her matter-of-fact question making him feel slightly dazed. 'Can I *what*?' he echoed in disbelief.

'Well, I can hardly ring for a lady-in-waiting to help me.' She looked at him, biting her lip. He wasn't exactly making it easy for her. 'Can I?'

Without a word, he turned and did as she asked, grateful for the fact that his back was towards her and she would not see the look of disbelief in his eyes. It wasn't the thought that someone might have walked in which so nagged at his conscience—no one would have *dared*—but more the fact that what had just taken place had been so…so…

So utterly inappropriate.

Was that why she had broken out of the mould she

must know was expected of her? Had she deliberately flirted with the young Italian to get just this reaction—to make him jealous enough to behave in a manner more befitting a sex-starved teenager than a king? And it had worked, damn her! It had worked!

He adjusted his clothing and walked back to where she lay, her legs still splayed, her colour all rosy. 'Here,' he said tightly, thrusting the tissues at her. 'You'd better hurry.'

She saw the brief but unmistakable glance at his watch and her cheeks flushed scarlet. It wasn't until she felt halfway decent again that she dared to broach what had just happened—for surely they couldn't just ignore the fact that they had just had sex in the middle of the day and in the middle of Gianferro's busy diary? And what of the jealousy which had started it— shouldn't that be addressed, too?

'It's pretty obvious from the look on your face that you wish we hadn't done that,' she said quietly.

Gianferro heard the unspoken plea for reassurance, but he didn't respond. He didn't want to discuss it, but to forget it and wipe it from his mind. And not just because he had let his guard down in such an inappropriate way—for how else was he to concentrate on the matters of State which lay stacked up and waiting for his attention?

'It happened, Millie. Nothing we can do about it now,' he said flatly, and with an effort he flashed her a smile. 'Don't you have a reception to attend?'

So he didn't want to discuss the underlying jealousy either. In fact, from the look on his face, he didn't want to discuss anything. She wondered if her face showed her disappointment.

It reminded Millie of the times when her father had still been alive, when he had returned from one of his interminably long trips abroad and Caius Hall would be bustling with anticipation of his arrival. Millie would be so excited, and would want to wait up to see him, but when he finally *did* arrive he would tell her that it was late and that he would see her in the morning. The memory of all that quashed excitement had never really left her. He had effectively dismissed her—just as Gianferro was doing now—and maybe it wasn't some crazy coincidence.

Was that what had made her fall for him? Had she done what they said all girls did—married a man who was the image of her father, because that was the only relationship she knew, one she felt familiar with?

She stood up and tugged down her dress, giving him a cool smile.

'You're right,' she murmured. 'I'd better dash.'

But he did not like her brittle either. He watched her walk towards the door, knowing that he must make compromises if this was to work, and yet compromise did not come easily to him. 'Millie?'

Composing her face, she turned back to him. 'Yes, Gianferro?'

'I meant what I said—about time for the two of us. Let's put dinner in the diary and let's make it a reg-

ular date. I'll speak to my secretary and he will speak
to yours.'

To anyone else it would have sounded mad, but to
Millie it was a small victory won. Time with her hus-
band. Just him. And her. 'How crazy that sounds.'
She giggled.

He nodded. 'I know.'

'Have…have a good day, darling.'

But Gianferro barely heard her. He had made his
small concession and now his dark head was bent.
Already he was preoccupied. He didn't even look up
as she opened the door—but then she doubted that he
had even heard her leave.

CHAPTER TEN

THE small change to their schedule seemed to have a knock-on effect within the relationship itself—though at first Millie was still insecure enough to put that down to wishful thinking.

But time changed her mind for her. Their allotted time together was precious—she'd spend the whole day looking forward to it, and she suspected that Gianferro did, too. There seemed something decadent about dismissing all the servants, and the sight of the King strolling into their apartment and unbuttoning his shirt with a wicked smile seemed like the fulfilment of her wildest fantasy!

For other couples it would doubtless be a huge treat to dine off golden plates and drink rare vintage wine. For her and Gianferro the opposite was true—it was simple food eaten with their fingers, while lolling around on the silken cushions which they dragged out onto the starlit terrace.

'Oh, I just love this,' said Millie dreamily one night. Her head was on her husband's bare chest and they were lying naked on the floor, washed in the moonlight which flooded into the room. In the distance she could see the dark glitter of the sea. 'Just

143

love it!' she emphasised as his hand moved to her breast.

Gianferro traced over her puckered nipple with the tip of his finger. 'I know you do. You make that abundantly clear, *cara.*'

'You're supposed to say, *So do I*!'

'Ah, but you know that to be true.'

'Then say it!'

He gave a mock frown. 'But if I say things you already know, then surely that would waste time. And since you tell me that we never have enough of it— then why would I want to do that?'

'Because…oh, Gianferro!' she gasped. 'Wh-what are you doing now?'

'What do you think I'm doing?' he purred, as he touched the tip of his tongue against her skin. Her head fell back.

The moon was very bright by the time he had rolled off her, and the stars were looped in the sky like Christmas tree lights. If only you could capture a moment and put it in a bottle—then this was the one she would choose. When they were alone and at peace.

When for a few brief hours their world and all its privilege retreated. It was as close to normality as they were ever likely to come.

Millie had come to realise something else… That maybe she had been wrong about not wanting a baby.

Maybe that was what happened automatically with women—the stronger your feelings for your partner grew, so too did the urge to have his child. She no longer saw it as a trap—in fact, if she was hands-on with their baby, as she intended to be, then wouldn't that be an even more normalising experience for the two of them to share?

She knew that Gianferro had told her Royal children should be brought up in a certain way, but his mind might now be open to change—just as it was over these evenings together. His life was rigidly defined, and Millie had come to recognise that change could only be achieved gradually and subtly—ultimately this stalling device on her part would benefit them both as a couple.

She touched her fingertips to his olive cheek, suddenly seeing all kinds of possibilities being opened up by her having a baby. Perhaps the fleetingly soft side she occasionally saw of her husband might be liberated by the birth of his own flesh and blood. She could but hope…

He whispered his lips across her hair, lazily touching her breast. 'I wonder if you're pregnant now,' he mused, and his voice deepened with longing. 'I wonder if what we have just done is the beginning of it all?'

In a way, this was nothing more than a variation on what he had said to her on their honeymoon, but the words no longer scared her. The way he said them had profoundly changed. It no longer sounded like an arrogant exercise in acquisition, but a heartfelt longing to have a child together. And his attitude had changed *her* attitude—of course it had.

But how did she go about telling him that she had come round to his way of thinking? That she had just needed time and space to come to terms with her new life?

'Hmm?' he whispered sleepily. Was it wrong to let a woman closer than he had ever done in the past? When his defences were down—did that make a man weak? 'What do you think, *cara mia*?'

'I wish I was pregnant,' she whispered back, and that was the truth. But the pain of what she had done—or failed to do—tore at her—tore at her like a ragged knife.

He no longer mentioned consulting a doctor, and she sensed that the urgency had left him. Maybe that was a direct result of their growing closeness. But what was she going to do about it?

Leaving Gianferro dozing, Millie rose to her feet and walked through the sumptuous rooms to the bathroom, but she didn't bother putting the main light on.

There were mirrors everywhere, and the light was surreal and silvered. Her dim reflection looked troubled. And she *was* troubled.

If she told him that she wanted to get pregnant now, that would mean telling him about the Pill…

The Millie of now was a different person from the innocent bride who had been daunted by her new position. It was so easy to recognise that she should have discussed contraception with her husband—but back then they had not been in a place to discuss anything. Gianferro had been so dogmatic and dominant and all-powerful, and she had had to fight for her part in his world.

Now she had made her own space there—true, it wasn't a very big one, but at least she had a foothold, and surely it could only get better.

She unzipped her make-up bag and looked down at the foil strip with some of the little circles punched out, which lay underneath a clutch of lipsticks. She knew that she ought to tell him. But something stopped her—and it was not just the fact that she now felt ashamed of what she had done. Wouldn't Gianferro feel a tremendous sense of hurt that she had excluded him from such a big decision—and wouldn't that have a detrimental effect on their growing relationship?

If only she had had the courage at the time—to stand up for what she believed in. But she had been barely twenty—thrown into a strange new world and struggling to find her own feet.

She stared at herself in the mirror, aware that her face looked older and more serious. As far as she could see she had two choices. Either she went in there and told him everything, or she simply stopped taking it. Gianferro would never know and would never need to feel hurt that she hadn't told him—and she might become pregnant straight away.

But something about doing that troubled her. Her deepening relationship with her husband would be much healthier if she was upfront and honest. If she told him and he was furious with her—well, he would be furious, and she would deserve it, but he would get over it.

The sense of knowing that this was somehow the right thing was enough to make her act decisively, and her fingers curled round the packet of Pills.

A movement distracted her, and she glanced up into the mirror, her heart leaping with something very close to fear when she saw Gianferro reflected there. He was standing in the doorway, as still and as watchful as a dark and brooding statue.

Now her heart began to race. 'Gianferro!' she cried. 'You startled me!'

'So I see.' He reached up and snapped on the light-switch. The room was flooded with bright fluorescent light, like a stage-set. 'What are you doing, Millie?'

But his voice didn't sound like his voice, and his question was spoken like an actor saying a line. Asking it because he knew it must be said, but knowing the answer because he had already read the script.

'I was just…just getting something out of my make-up bag.'

'And what something is that?'

With a cold feeling of dread Millie realised that he knew. Her mouth felt so dry that it felt as if it was cracking inside. 'My P-pills,' she stumbled. She looked into his eyes and almost recoiled from the stony look she saw there. 'You saw?'

'Of course I saw,' he said icily.

'I know what it must look like,' she said quickly, 'but I was going to stop taking them. Tonight. I was just going to bring them into the sitting room to show you before I threw them away!'

'What an extraordinary coincidence!' he drawled sarcastically.

'I know what it must sound like, but it's true.'

'I don't believe you,' he said coldly.

She saw the light go out in his eyes, and something inside her began to scream with pain. And panic. 'It is. Honestly—'

'*Honestly?*' His mouth hardened into a look of utter disdain. 'How dare you use that word?' he raged. 'How *dare* you use it to me?'

'Gianferro—I realise how it must seem—'

'Oh, please, Millie.' The breath he sucked in felt as though it had been fired into his lungs by a flame-thrower. He had not known that it was possible to feel such a hot sense of injustice. 'I have had my suspicions—so please don't heap insult onto injury by attempting some kind of false apology.'

She stared at him. 'Your...*suspicions*?' she breathed. 'You mean you suspected?'

His eyes were like black ice. 'Of course I suspected—what kind of fool do you take me for?' he snapped. The kind of fool who had not wanted to frighten or to hurt her with his nebulous fears—when all the time it seemed he had been right to harbour them. Now he wanted to lash out. He wanted to hurt her back, as she had hurt him—and to salvage something of his pride, too, to show her that he was not a fool, and that she had badly underestimated him.

Oh, so very badly...

But he had let her, hadn't he? When questions had drifted into his mind he had chosen to ignore them... because he'd wanted to believe that his young wife was pure and sweet and true. Because the alternative had been unthinkable.

He had blithely ignored all the dangers of letting a woman get close and he had misjudged her. Just because a woman was a virgin that didn't mean that she couldn't also be a liar and a cheat. He had forgiven her for the understandable lapse with the Italian teacher, and yet all the time there had been this far greater sin of deception waiting in the wings.

'In some corner of my mind I have suspected for some time,' he said furiously, but part of his rage was directed at himself. For letting her innocence blind him to what was crashingly obvious. Well, *more fool you*, he told himself bitterly.

Millie's heart was breaking as she saw the look of contempt on his face—but worse than that was the fact that she had been deluding herself. She had thought that their relationship was deepening, that they were growing closer all the time. She had allowed herself to bask in the confidence that what they had between them would soon be strong enough to provide a secure base for a baby. But it seemed she had been wrong. How wrong?

She screwed up her eyes. 'But...but how? How on earth could you know?'

'Oh, come on, Millie! A woman who shares her

husband's desire to have a baby usually exhibits some kind of disappointment each month when it does not happen. But not you.' His eyes gleamed coldly as the stealthy poison of betrayal began to seep in. 'Oh, no. You used to answer my questions with the air of someone who had always known what the answer would be…because of course you damned well did! You had already made certain what the answer would be.'

Her lips trembled. 'Won't you please let me explain?'

'What's to explain? That you deceived me?' he bit out, and he saw her flinch but didn't care. He didn't *care*. For the first time in his life he had been guilty of brushing a suspicion aside because he hadn't wanted to believe it. And the fact that his judgement had failed him wounded his ego and his pride as much as anything else. 'Because, no matter how much you try to dress it up, that is the truth of it,' he bit out.

But her words rushed out anyway, tumbling over themselves in an effort to explain. To try and get him to understand—even though deep down she feared that it was too late for understanding. Oh, why had she done it—and then, having done it, left it so long? Because that was what happened sometimes. You were troubled by a nagging fear and it just seemed easier to brush it aside. Well, she was about to pay for it.

With her marriage?

'I just felt that we were rushing into parenthood.

That it was too soon to have a child between us when we didn't really know each other as people. Gianferro—you wondered out loud on our *honeymoon* whether you had made me pregnant!'

'And how you must have laughed,' he said softly. 'Because presumably you were already on the Pill.'

'Yes! But I didn't laugh—of course I didn't. I was scared. And mixed-up, if you must know—because I had been to see my doctor and he had prescribed me the Pill as a matter of course. I understood that was what all brides-to-be did.'

'You didn't think of discussing it with *me* first?' he demanded.

'How could I—when the subject was so clearly off-limits? You married me because I fulfilled certain criteria, and the main one was my innocence! So you can hardly expect me to have brought up the subject of birth control with you before the wedding, can you? Even if I'd wanted to—or dared to—we were scarcely alone for a second!'

'How about afterwards, Millie? Huh? Once we had been…intimate? Couldn't you have told me then?'

She knew that it would muddy the waters still further to tell him that intimacy had been a long time in coming for her that only recently had she really felt they had finally reached it.

'You frightened me with your autocratic assurance that we should have a child straight away,' she admitted. 'I felt as though I would shrink for ever into the shadows if I did.'

'Oh, what is the point in all this?' he bit out impatiently. 'We could go round and round in circles for ever, and in the meantime I could use my time more usefully.'

'More *usefully*?' she echoed in disbelief.

He wanted to hurt her as badly as she had hurt him, and he lashed out now as only he could. Nothing so coarse as personal insults, but words dipped in the icy and distancing substance of Court protocol. 'If you will excuse me, Millie—I have matters which require my attention.'

'You still don't understand, do you?' she questioned slowly.

He gave her a look of imperial disdain and Millie almost shrank. 'Are you trying to suggest that I'm missing the point?' He raised his dark brows. 'Perhaps it was less a fear of pregnancy itself which was the problem—but concern about the identity of the father.'

'*What?*'

He shrugged. 'It is possible that your tutor's insinuations about the extent of your relationship were based on truth rather than fantasy.'

'Now you're just being ridiculous!'

'You think so?' He shook his head and raised his eyebrows in autocratic query. 'Everything suddenly looks very different when you discover that your partner has been living a lie. Tell me, Millie—did you imagine me to be such a tyrant that I would *insist* on you carrying a baby if the idea was so abhorrent to you?'

'N-no—but I didn't think you'd understand my fears.'

'Just your long-term deceit?' He shook his head as he opened the door. 'In that case, my dear—you have been a fool.'

Her head and her thoughts were spinning. Nothing seemed coherent or real any more, and the look of contempt in his black eyes told her that even if she did manage to explain how she had felt at the time he probably wouldn't believe her. He didn't *want* to believe her.

'Where are you going?' she asked him miserably.

'Out.'

'And when are you coming back?'

'I have no idea,' he snapped. 'And even if I did—it is none of your business.'

'Gianferro—please don't do this—please don't shut me out.'

His dark eyes were incredulous as they looked at her. 'How do you…*you*…have the nerve to say that to me, Millie?'

It was like when you dropped a leaf into a fast-flowing river as a child, and the current carried it far, far away, and you didn't know where—that was what was happening to them now. Her actions had prompted it, and he didn't want to fight it.

She wanted to ask him—was a person not allowed to make one mistake? But that might sound like begging, and in her heart she knew that he would despise that, too. If he wasn't going to forgive her, then she couldn't force him—but maybe if she put some space between them it might help him to try. Give him a chance for him to see how he really felt. And a chance for her, too, to come to terms with the fact that he might not want her any more.

'You once suggested that I might like to take a trip back to England?' she said slowly.

'Homesick, are you, Millie?' he scorned softly.

His attitude swung it. She was already isolated by her position and her age—but before she had always had the support of her husband. If he now withdrew it, she would be left with nothing.

Nothing.

'A little,' she agreed, wanting to save face and not to finish with a blazing row which would leave a bitter memory. 'Would that be possible?'

Her gaze was very steady as she looked at him. Was half of her praying that he would change his mind? Try to talk her out of it or come with her?

He stared at her. Outwardly she looked just as beautiful as when he had first met her—with her long blonde hair and blue eyes, and her skin which was as soft as silk-satin. But she had changed—he saw that now, as if for the first time.

She wore the air of a sexually confident woman, and he had liberated that in her. He had made her into his perfect lover; and supposedly his perfect wife as well—only now he had discovered that it had all been an elaborate sham. The girl of such simple tastes had gone for ever and he had been instrumental in making her that way. She had grown up.

And even if he could bring himself to forgive her—didn't her actions speak about more than simply the fear of having children? In a way, hadn't part of her been rejecting Royal life—because she had been in no position to reject it before, not until she had actually been exposed to it? And was that not her prerogative? Far better she did it when there was no child to complicate things even further?

But he was unprepared for the dark torrent of pain which swept over him. He was relieved when it passed and was replaced by the emptiness he was so familiar with. In a way he felt comfortable with that. He knew where he was with that feeling, for it had been with him all his life.

He stared at her as if he was looking at her for the first time. Or maybe the last. 'I will speak to Alesso about arranging a flight as soon as possible,' he said.

The anger had left his voice and been replaced with a kind of bleakness, and in a way that was much, much worse.

The last thing Millie saw before the door closed behind him were his shoulders, which had unconsciously girded themselves to face the prying eyes of the world outside, and she was left staring after him through a blur of tears, utterly heartbroken at what she had done to him.

CHAPTER ELEVEN

MILLIE stared out of the window at the familiar green landscape softened by water—a mixture of the steady rain which fell and the tears which were filling her eyes.

'It all looks exactly the same,' she said brokenly. 'Nothing changes.'

'But you've changed,' said Lulu, from behind her. 'You're almost unrecognisable.'

'Am I?' Millie turned round, her sense of surprise momentarily eclipsing the terrible pain she had felt since setting foot back in her old family home. 'But my hair is the same and my face is the same. The clothes are more expensive, and I may have lost a little weight—but that's about all.'

'Maybe the profound experience of marrying and becoming a queen almost simultaneously has altered you more than you realised? Oh, Millie—don't! Please don't start crying again!'

But Millie couldn't help it. She had bottled her feelings up—not wanting the servants to see her giving in to emotion—that had been one lesson which Gianferro had taught her so well. But once away from the closed environment of the Palace which had become her home the tears had begun to fall in earnest, and now they were splashing down onto her cashmere sweater, which she hugged close to her, like an animal seeking comfort.

'I just don't understand what the problem is.' Lulu stared at her in confusion. 'You didn't bother telling him you were on the Pill—is it really such a big deal?' she asked.

Millie bit her lip. She had thought that coming here might help put everything in perspective, but in a way it had only emphasised the gravity of what she had done. It was more than simply not telling her husband something—it was the severing of a trust which he gave to very few people.

But he suspected you, she reminded herself. He told you that himself. So he did not trust you at all.

'I just don't know what to do!' she whispered.

'Well, stop crying, for a start! Just calm down and take a deep breath.' Lulu's face was very fierce. 'It's not the end of the world.'

'But what if it's the end of my marriage?' questioned Millie shakily.

Lulu's eyes narrowed. 'Would that bother you?'

Millie scrubbed at her eyes with her fingers. 'Of course it would bother me!'

'Because you like being Queen?'

'No, you idiot—because I love him! How dare you suggest a thing like that?'

Lulu went quiet for a moment. 'Well, thank God for that. I just had to be sure, that's all. Sure you knew what you were fighting for.'

Millie turned her head to look at the rainwashed lawn. 'Maybe Gianferro doesn't want to be fought for. Maybe he's decided that it's over.'

'You're going to give in that easily? Whatever happened to the Millie who would never give up? Who got back on her horse again and again—no matter how many times she had fallen off?'

Millie listened to Lulu in silence and realised that her sister was right. That even if he *had* decided he didn't want her any more, she had to give it another chance. She had to. She would fight with every fibre of her being if that was what it took.

'I'm going to have to go back to Mardivino and sort it out,' she said slowly. 'Because he's certainly showing no sign of coming to England to find *me*.'

Lulu raised her eyebrows. 'Oh, come on!' she chided. 'How can he? What? Hop on a plane and arrive here unannounced? He's the *King*, Millie—and kings just don't do that kind of thing!'

He could, Millie thought—could have done it if he had wanted to. Because he had the power at his fingertips to do almost anything he wanted. The point was that he didn't want to—and who on earth could blame him?

She felt the cold, curling fingers of pain clamping themselves around her heart, but to stay in a state of confused ignorance would never help her heart to heal. Her marriage might be over, and the sooner she learned the truth about it, the better. And Lulu was right... Why should she give up when nothing in the world had ever been so worth fighting for as this man was?

Millie had travelled on a scheduled flight, but after a week in England with no word at all from Gianferro she was feeling tired and vulnerable. She couldn't face the thought of returning to Mardivino by the same route—with the VIP representatives fussing and hovering round her at the airport, the inevitable lurking paparazzo photographer lurking around to snatch a photo of the young Queen.

She had not anticipated how greedy the press would be for images of her—or how carefully she would need to plan her wardrobe for travelling. One hint of a loose-fitting top and it would be announced to the world that she was pregnant. Millie bit her lip. How ironic.

She phoned the Palace, but Gianferro and Alesso were not there.

Eventually Millie got through to Alesso on his cell-phone. 'Is Gianferro there?' she asked him quietly.

'He is touring the new hospital.'

'I see. Well, I want to come home…' For a second she was aware that she no longer considered England as her home—it should have been a small victory of her newly married life, but it tasted bitterly of defeat. 'Can you arrange for the King's flight to be sent for me, Alesso?'

'Yes, of course, Your Majesty.'

'And Alesso? Will you tell him I rang?' she said

quietly and then her voice softened. 'And that I shall see him tomorrow evening.'

'Yes, Your Majesty.'

While Millie's lady-in-waiting packed for her, she and Lulu wandered down to the stables, and as they stood looking down at a brand-new foal Millie was overcome with a powerful wave of nostalgia for how things used to be—when life had seemed a whole lot simpler.

'Do you miss England?' asked Lulu suddenly, when they had walked back through the fields, splashing through the boggy puddles in their Wellington boots. The sun had emerged from behind a cloud and its brightness was drying all the leaves on the branches, like washing hung on a line.

Millie closed her eyes and breathed in the very Englishness of the air. Her senses could transport her back to other times and other places, and never more so than now, when her senses were so keenly alert. But nothing did stay the same—it might look the same on the outside, but the people who flitted in and out were growing and changing all the time. 'Sometimes.'

'But not the weather?' joked Lulu.

'No, not the weather.' Millie smiled.

'What, then?'

'Oh, the freedom. Yes, the freedom, mainly—being able to do what you want without consulting a diary or a secretary. Being able to wander off without men in bulky jackets never being very far away from you.

But that's life as a Royal—and I knew that when I married Gianferro.'

But in a way she had known it only on a purely intellectual level—she had been unprepared for the reality of almost complete loss of freedom. She had floundered in her new life, like a little squirming fish thrown into a mighty swirling ocean. And instead of turning to her husband for help and support she had pushed him away—driven a wedge between them with her stubbornness and the secret she had nursed.

Was it too late to try and get close to him again?

The private jet skated onto the runway at Solajoya airport the following day and Millie stared out of the window, hoping and praying for the sight of her husband come to meet her—but there was no sign of him.

Not even Alesso was there—just a couple of officials who Millie did not know terribly well. She had not wanted a fuss, but she had expected *some* kind of welcome—no matter how lukewarm. But this felt like…like what? As if she was being marginalised? As if a very definite message was being sent out to her?

Her feelings of insecurity grew all the way to the Palace, and once there things were no better, for there was no sign of the King. No note. Nothing.

Nothing.

Millie kicked the shoes off her aching feet and looked around the empty suite of rooms. Nor were there any flowers on the tables. The shutters were drawn as if nobody lived there any more, and she moved forward to open them so that golden sunlight poured like honey into the room, leaving her dazzled and confused as she turned to her dresser.

'Has there been any word on when the King might return, Flavia?'

'No, Your Majesty.'

She picked up the phone. Gianferro was not answering his mobile, but then he rarely did. It was Alesso that she got through to. As usual.

'You had a good flight, Your Majesty?' he enquired.

'Yes, yes,' answered Millie impatiently. 'Where are you?'

'In Soloroca—it is the anniversary of the opening of the Juan Lopez Gallery, remember?'

'Is Gianferro not there with you?'

'Unfortunately, no. He has taken the Spanish officials sailing.'

Millie scowled at her reflection in the mirror. 'And what time is he expected back at the Palace tonight?'

There was an almost infinitesimal pause. 'There is a reception which is not scheduled to end until late, Your Majesty. The King gave the instruction that he may be delayed and that you are not to wait up for him.'

There were a million things she wanted to say, but she could not. Alesso knew as well as she did that the King could leave any reception at any damned time he pleased—if he did not do so, it was because he had chosen not to. His wife had been away for over a week and he wasn't even going to bother to see her until the next day. Which told her in no uncertain terms just how much he cared.

Millie felt her heart plummet, as if someone had dropped it from the top of a very high building. She knew that so much in Royal life was never stated, that things were 'understood'. It saved embarrassment—and presumably little could be more embarrassing than having to tell your young wife that their brief marriage was over.

But was she going to sit back and accept that?

Millie stared at herself in the mirror and her scowl became a look of fierce determination, her blue eyes glinting and her chin held high. For sure she had made a mistake—but wasn't everybody allowed one mistake without it having such an irrevocable effect on their lives?

But she knew her husband's Achilles' heel—anything which threatened his strong sense of duty would be just that. He would not want his marriage to fail for the sake of his people—no matter what his personal feelings for her.

And Millie did not want her marriage to fail either—though her reasons were fundamentally different. So was she going to fight for him? To show him what he meant to her? That she loved him with a love that burned deep in her breast like an eternal flame?

Yes, she was!

The first thing she did was strip off all her travelling clothes and shower, soaping her body and her hair as if her life depended on it and then rubbing rich scented lotion into her skin afterwards, so that she was perfumed and gleaming. The faint golden colour she had acquired since living on the island made her eyes look very blue, and her hair was paler than it had been for a long time.

She chose her lingerie carefully, and a simple dress of lemon silk, and caught her hair back in a French twist—weaving into it a ribbon the colour of buttercups.

The next bit was the tricky part. She had to persuade her bodyguard to let her drive a car, unaccompanied and unannounced. She saw the furrowed lines of worry which creased his brow and sought to reassure him.

'I don't mean completely on my own! You can follow me,' she told him. 'I want to surprise my husband,' she finished, and gave him a smile which was tinged with genuine pleading.

And of course she got her way—short of refusing the Queen's command, what alternative did the bodyguard have? Millie rarely used the full power of her title, but this time it was vital.

If the purpose of the drive hadn't been so crucial to her future happiness then she might even have embraced the feeling of freedom and exhilaration as the zippy little car began to ascend the mountain roads outside the capital.

This was the kind of thing she never did—it was

always a big chauffeur-driven limousine with the Royal crest on the front which conveyed her to and from her Royal engagements. But this felt…

Normal.

Ordinary.

All those things Gianferro had reminded her that she no longer was, nor ever would be again.

Maybe not. But the feelings she had were the same as those experienced by ordinary people, weren't they?

And right now the overwhelming one was fear. That it might be too late. That she had messed it up.

Licking at lips so dry they felt like parchment, Millie drove upwards. At least the way was well sign-posted. Gianferro had told her that the road to Soloroca had once been little more than a track, and the village itself had been rundown and desolate—but that had been before the works of the great artist Juan Lopez had been housed there, and now people came from all over the world to view them, bringing prosperity to the mountains of Mardivino.

She waited until she was on the outskirts of the village and then she telephoned Alesso.

'I'm here,' she said.

'Here, Your Majesty?'

'Just down the road, in fact.' Millie drew a deep breath. 'Alesso, I want the way cleared for me to come to the reception, but I do not wish Gianferro to know. I want to surprise him, so please don't tell him.'

'But, Your Majesty—'

'*Please*, Alesso.'

There was a pause. 'Very well, Your Majesty.'

It was a mark of how much Royal life had seeped into her unconscious that her first thought had been to clear it with her husband's aide. For, while many would recognise her as the Queen, others might have considered her to be an impostor—there could have been an almighty fuss, and then the crucial element of surprise would have been lost.

And she wanted to see Gianferro's first instinctive reaction to her. Oh, he was a master at keeping his face poker-straight and expressionless, but surely his eyes would give *some* kind of reaction. Even if there was the tiniest bit of pleasure lurking in their black depths, then surely that was enough to build on?

And if there was no pleasure? What then?

Millie quickly smoothed her hair and straightened her back. She was not going to project an outcome.

Her way might have been prepared by Alesso—for all the guards bowed as if they had been expecting her—but that did not mean there were not curious eyes in the room. Older, predatory married women, who were always in evidence around the King, were fixing her with unwelcome eyes. Millie knew that many of them were just itching to step into her shoes. To provide the King with the physical comfort a man of his appetite needed—with no questions asked and no demands made.

Did he still want his foolish young wife? Millie

wondered, her eyes searching the high-domed white room whose walls were lined with the vibrant paintings of Lopez.

And then she saw him.

He was wearing a dark suit and looked both cool and formal. As usual, all heads were bent obsequiously towards him as people listened, and Millie knew that if he made a joke—however weak—people would fall about laughing. Because when you were King people told you what they thought you wanted to hear.

She knew then that her attempt at reconciliation must go no further than was necessary—for if she capitulated too much he would never respect her again.

He might be King, and she Queen, but the tussles within their marriage were not Royal ones—and unless they could find some real human ground on which to thrash them out then it would not be a marriage worth continuing with anyway.

Gianferro was listening to the Spanish Ambassador praising Mardivino's attitude to the arts when he became aware of a slight buzz in the room. His eyes narrowed as he saw heads turning in the direction of the door.

But he was already in the room! Who in the world could possibly be entering and capturing more attention than he could?

And then he saw her.

Her eyes were like a summer's sky and her hair as pale and gleaming as moonlight. She wore a yellow dress which made her look cool and composed, but he could see that her mouth was set and tense, though it wavered in a tentative attempt at a smile as she began to walk towards him.

Now the faces were turned towards him, watching for his reaction, the way they always did. They would be wondering what the Queen was doing here, for she was not expected—and members of the Royal family did not simply turn up out of the blue.

What the hell was she thinking of? he wondered angrily.

She moved towards him and the purely physical reaction which she always provoked in him kicked in—with a force and power which momentarily took his breath away. But then he remembered the ugly scene which had caused her departure, and he felt the faint flickering of a muscle at his cheek.

She came right up to him, her cheeks flushed and her eyelids dropping down to conceal the sapphire glitter of her eyes.

'Your Majesty,' she said, very softly.

And, breaking protocol for the first time in his life, Gianferro bent his mouth to her ear.

'What the hell are you doing here?' he breathed.

CHAPTER TWELVE

MILLIE felt faint and dizzy—her heart was beating so loudly that it threatened to deafen her as she looked into the cold and unwelcoming eyes of Gianferro— but somehow she managed to keep a small and noncommittal smile pinned to her mouth. People were watching them—she dared not let her fragile emotions show.

'Are you not pleased to see me, Gianferro?'

With an equally non-committal smile, he placed his palm beneath her elbow.

'Surprised,' he murmured. And that was an understatement. The last thing he had expected was to see his beautiful blonde wife slinking across the reception room towards him, and for once he was unprepared. Fleetingly he allowed himself to wonder how a normal man might have dealt with such a situation, but the eyes of the room were fixed on them.

Damn her! Had she deliberately contrived to catch him off-guard? To slip beneath his defences as cunningly as she always managed to do in bed? When she made him feel like Samson after his hair had been shorn? Had he not spent the past week telling himself over and over that she must not be allowed to do so again?

'I will speak with you in private, my dear,' he continued. 'But first I must make my farewells.'

His voice was soft, but the words were undoubtedly a command, and something in the dark glitter of his eyes made Millie suddenly apprehensive.

'I didn't intend to drag you away,' she whispered.

'Really? Then just what *did* you intend, Millie? That you would flounce in here unannounced and everyone would just pretend not to notice?'

It was a reprimand, and one she knew she deserved. 'What do you want me to do?'

But at that moment, as if summoned by some unspoken order, Alesso appeared. Gianferro spoke to him rapidly and fiercely in Italian, and then he bent his head to her ear once more.

'Go now with Alesso,' he said, switching effortlessly to English. 'And wait for me. It will only complicate matters if formal introductions are made,' he added coolly. 'At least this way the Spanish Ambassador can be reliably informed that there is a family crisis.'

And was there? Millie wondered, as she followed Alesso from the room, pride making her smile at the people who bowed and curtsied as she passed. Of course there was...and by the time she and Gianferro were through maybe the Palace lawyers would have been instructed to draw up the papers announcing a formal separation.

In the corridor, she saw Alesso's look of resignation.

'I've got you into trouble, haven't I?' she guessed.

'He is not pleased.'

Millie bit her lip. 'I'm sorry, Alesso.'

He shook his head. 'No. It is for the best. I do not like to see the King miserable. He cannot rule with so much on his mind.'

'How has he been?' Millie asked breathlessly, wondering if Alesso would give her any inkling of the truth, or just be Gianferro's official mouthpiece.

'Distracted,' he admitted with a shrug.

And Millie wondered what he had been distracted with. Had he missed her? Or had he simply been working out the best and cleanest way to end the marriage? 'Is there somewhere very private we could go?'

He nodded. 'It is already arranged. The Cacciatore family own a house on the coastal road. He is taking you there. It is empty and—'

But at that moment Gianferro himself swept out, accompanied by a retinue of diplomats and servants. His black eyes gave little away as he looked at Millie other than faint displeasure, but he could not stem the sudden rush of blood to his groin. He found himself thinking how much more uncomplicated life was without a woman in it, and his mouth hardened.

'Come,' he said crisply.

As she slid into the back of the large unmarked car beside him she told herself that this was never going to be a romantic reunion. But his proximity sent her already raw senses into overdrive. She was achingly aware of him as a man—of the long, lean thrust of his legs and the muscular body so tightly coiled beside her. Could he not have touched her? At least reached out to squeeze the frozen fingers which looked so lifeless where they lay against the lemon silk dress.

Gianferro was aware of a mixture of powerlessness and frustration—of wanting to press her body hard against his and knowing that the presence of the driver ruled it out. But it was more than that. He still did not know why she was here—her very eagerness to confront him might spell her determination to seek a new life for herself.

Could he blame her if she did?

The silence between them grew as the powerful car ate up the miles, and Millie didn't know whether to be relieved or terrified when a pair of electric gates opened and their car was spotlighted by the security lighting which zapped on.

She wasn't really aware of the terse conversation going on between Gianferro and his head of security, only that it seemed to take endless negotiations before the two of them were finally alone in a rather formal-looking salon. It had the air of a room which had not been lived in for some time—although the furniture was very beautiful indeed.

Gianferro closed the door quietly and an immense silence seemed to swallow them up. He looked at her properly then, as if for the first time, but his face did not relax.

'So, Millie,' he said quietly, 'is there some kind of explanation for this extraordinary behaviour?'

She stared at him, bewildered and hurt. 'I wanted to see you.'

'And now you have.'

'You aren't going to make this easy for me, are you, Gianferro?'

He gave her the bland, formal smile she had seen him use at so many official functions. 'Make what easy?'

She wanted to drum her fists against his chest, to tell him that he couldn't hide behind that icy persona—except that she knew he could. Had she thought that simply because she had seen it melt from time to time it was gone for ever? Of course it wasn't.

She looked at him. 'I'm so sorry for what I did, my darling,' she whispered. 'And I wondered...' She swallowed down the lump in her throat and the salty taste of tears which tainted her mouth. 'Maybe I have no right to ask this—but do you think you can ever find it in your heart to forgive me?'

Her words touched him as he had not expected or wanted to be touched, and so did her stricken face, but he steeled his heart against her. 'I don't know,' he said tonelessly.

Millie felt as if he had struck her, but she remained strong. Maybe what had happened between them was too big to be cured with just a single word of apology. Maybe he didn't want it to be cured.

She bit her lip. 'Do you want to save our marriage?'

A cold and sardonic smile curved his lips. It had been his trademark smile as a bachelor, and he was discovering how easy it was to slip back into it. But this nagging ache in his heart had never been there in those days, which seemed so long ago now. 'Is it worth saving, do you think, Millie?'

She told herself that he was deliberately trying to hurt her, and that she must withstand his taunts. That this, in a way, was her punishment. And she *wanted* to suffer, for she had made him suffer, and then she wanted to be washed clean of all her pain and regret and to start all over again. But this might be one idealistic hope too far, it could only work if he wanted it, too.

'Yes,' she said, in a low, firm voice. 'Yes, I do. More than anything.'

And then she knew that she had to do something else, too. That it was foolish for her to wait for words of love from Gianferro. Even if he *did* feel love— which she doubted—he would be unable to show it, for nobody had shown him *how* to. This wasn't some quiz from a women's magazine. It didn't *matter* who said what and in what order. Just because some ancient code said that the man was supposed to declare his feelings first she didn't have to heed it! If it was just pride standing in the way of her telling him how she really felt—then what good was pride?

What good was anything if she didn't have her

man? And didn't she owe it to Gianferro to tell him
how much he meant to her?

'I think it's worth saving because when I made my
vows I meant them. I think it's worth saving because
I have a duty both to you and to Mardivino, to provide
emotional security and succour to their King.'

She swallowed down the last of her fears as she
looked up into his face with very clear and bright blue
eyes. 'But, most important of all, I think it's worth
saving because I love you, Gianferro, even though
you think I may not have shown it. I have loved you
for a long, long time now, but I have never dared tell
you. And now I am terrified that my stupid actions
will prevent me from ever showing you just how
much.'

He stilled. What she was offering was like a beacon
glowing on a dark night. It was comfort from the
storm and warmth in the depths of winter. It was like
having walked in the desert for days and being
tempted with the sight of an oasis shimmering on the
horizon. But Gianferro had walked for too long alone
to allow himself to give in to temptation. She was
offering him an easier, softer option, and he didn't
need one—he didn't *need her*.

He should tell her to go to hell. He should tell her
that he could live without her. And he could. He had
before and he would again.

His heart was pounding with the pumped-up feelings of a man about to enter battle. But as he looked
at her he realised that he did not want to do battle

with her. He continued to stare at her, remembering the slight figure and the fearlessness which had first so entranced him. Then she had been a tomboy, but today she looked regal and beautiful. In her eyes he could read that self-same fearlessness, but now there was doubt, too.

'You would recover if it ended,' he said harshly.

She shook her head. 'Not properly. Only on the surface.'

'And you would find another man.'

'But never like you,' she said simply. 'And you know that. You told me that once yourself, on the very day you proposed marriage to me.'

Gianferro's eyes narrowed as he remembered. So he had! Even on that day he had used an arrogant persuasion which could almost be defined as subtle force. He had been determined to have her and he had gone all out to get her. She hadn't stood a chance.

He had brought her here and then told her—*told* her—that she should have his child immediately, when she had still been so very young and inexperienced herself.

Was that the kind of tyrant he had become? So used to imposing his will that he didn't stop to think about whether it was appropriate to do so with his new wife?

Pain crossed his face as for the first time he acknowledged where his arrogance and pride could lead him if he let it. To a life alone. An empty life. A life without her. His life was one into which she had crept like a flame, bringing both warmth and light into it. Her absence had left a dull, aching gap behind—even though the independent side of him had resented that.

He had once seen her as a path to be taken in a hazy landscape, but now he could see very clearly the two paths which lay before him. He saw what being with his wife would mean, and more terrifyingly, he saw what being without her promised. A life which would be stark and empty and alone.

'Oh, Millie,' he said brokenly. 'Millie.'

The face she turned up to him was wreathed in anxiety and fear. 'Gianferro?' she breathed, in a voice she prayed would not dissolve into tears. Something in his expression gave her a tenuous hope, but she was too scared to hang onto it in case it was false. 'Just tell me—and if you really want it to be over then I will accept that. I will never like it, nor will I ever stop loving you, but I will do as you wish.'

Something in her words let the floodgates open, and feeling came flooding in to wash over the barren landscape of his heart. After a lifetime of being kept at bay it was sharp and bright and painful and warm, all at the same time, and Gianferro gave a small gasp of bewilderment—he who had never known a moment's doubt in his life.

He pulled her into his arms and looked down at her, not quite knowing where to begin. He had never had to say sorry to anyone in his life, and now he began to recognise that it had not done him any favours. He realised that he was more than just a symbol of power, a figurehead. Inside, his heart beat the same as that of any other man. And having feelings didn't make you weak, he realised—not if it could make you feel as alive as he felt right at that moment. Cut yourself adrift from them and you were not a complete person—and how could he rule unless he was?

'It is me who should be begging your forgiveness,' he said quietly. 'For living in the Dark Ages and refusing to make this a modern marriage. For thinking that I could impose my will on you as if you were simply one of my subjects, forgetting—or choosing to ignore—the fact that you are my wife. My partner. My Millie.'

'Oh, Gianferro!'

'I was a tyrant!' he whispered.

'Not all the time.'

He smiled. 'But some of the time?'

'Well, yes. But then, I have my own faults and failings that I must live with and deal with.' Shadows danced across her face, and then she looked up at him, her eyes clear and blue and questioning. 'What will we do?'

'We will begin again. What else can we do, *cara* Millie? As of today we will move forward, not back.'

Her heart felt as if it was going to burst with joy, and all the dark and terrible fantasies about what *could* have happened began to dissolve. Never again, she decided, was she going to take the coward's way out—of hiding her doubts and her fears and letting them grow. From this day forward there would be the transparency of true love. From her, at least. And she was not going to ask anything of Gianferro. Not push him or manipulate him into saying anything that he didn't mean. But she had to know something.

'Does that mean we can still be married, then?' she questioned shakily.

And Gianferro burst out laughing as he lifted her chin and allowed the love which blazed from her eyes to light him with its warmth. Why had she never looked at him that way before? *Because she was scared to.* He kissed the tip of her nose with lips which were tender. 'Oh, yes, my love,' he replied softly. 'Yes, we can still be married.'

She tightened her arms around his back. 'Kiss me.'

He grazed his lips against hers. 'Like this?'

'More.'

'Like this, perhaps?'

Millie gasped. 'Oh, yes. Yes. Just like that.'

He carried her upstairs and made love to her on the silken counterpane of some unknown bed, and it was better than anything she had ever known because now she was free to really show him how much she cared. She began to cry out in helpless wonder, and he gasped too, then bent his head to kiss her, until her cries were spent and her body had stopped shuddering in time with his.

Millie ran her fingertips down the side of his lean face, aware that her next words were going to remind him of what she had done—or failed to do—but she was never going to shrink from the difficult things in life again.

'I'm going to chuck my Pills away—'

'No.' He shook his head. 'No, that is precisely what you are not going to do, *cara*.'

In the moonlight, she stared at him in confusion. 'But, Gianferro, you want an heir—'

'So I do,' he agreed gently. 'But you are only twenty, Millie, and I want us to have time together first. To learn about each other. To learn to love one another.'

To *learn* to love. If she had heard that only hours ago it would have hurt, but Millie had done a lot of growing up in those hours. She had had to—her marriage had depended on it. And life wasn't always like the fairy story you longed it to be. Love didn't always strike you like a thunderbolt—though lust did! Sometimes it had its basis in all kinds of things you didn't understand. Two people could instinctively reach out for one another on a level which would confound common sense—and that was what had happened to her and Gianferro—but after that you had to work at it.

It was like riding. You could love horses with a mad passion, but you couldn't possibly learn to ride without being thrown off!

'We will have a baby when it is time to have a baby,' he said, and bent his lips to brush them over hers. 'And in the meantime—what is it that they say?'

His eyes glittered with mischief. 'We will have fun... practising.'

Oh, yes, she thought, as he pulled her against him once more. You can say that again.

EPILOGUE

MILLIE learned the hard way that babies were not something that could be ordered up—like strawberries on a summer menu.

She and Gianferro had a year to themselves before they ceremonially threw her Pills away while he wiped her tears of regret with soft and healing kisses. A year of exploring and learning about each other, learning how to live as husband and wife. And how to love. But that bit came more easily than either of them had expected—especially where Gianferro was concerned. It was as though, having given himself permission, he entered into loving with the true zeal of the convert. Passion had always come easily to him, and so now did love.

Millie was having formal language lessons, and she got her husband to speak to her in French and Spanish, and Alesso in Italian, and gradually she was picking up a smattering of all three.

It helped that she had nephews and nieces who were fluent in all the languages spoken on Mardivino—and she had made a big effort to befriend their mothers. Their slight diffidence towards her had quickly worn off, and once they'd seen that she wasn't just going through the motions of friendship Ella and

Lucy had welcomed her into their families with open arms. And for the first time since he had been a little boy Gianferro had begun to get to know his two brothers properly.

In fact, everything was absolutely perfect except on the baby front—because nothing had happened. After months of trying, she still wasn't pregnant, and Millie didn't know what to do about it. She didn't dare ask anyone else about *their* experiences—not even her sisters-in-law—because she didn't want anyone else to know. It was too big a deal for everyone concerned. She wasn't like other women. Once she went to the doctor it would be on record, and then…

But what if…?

'Why are you frowning so?' Gianferro asked one night, as they were getting dressed for dinner.

Millie had once made a vow to herself that she would not shirk responsibility, but she was unprepared for the pain of voicing *these* fears—and even more concerned about the possible consequences if they happened to be true.

'I'm not pregnant,' she said.

'I'd rather guessed that.'

Her head shot up. 'How?' And then she saw the silent laughter in his black eyes, and blushed. 'Gianferro—it's not funny—what if…what if…?'

'What if you can't have a baby?'

'Well, yes!' She put her hairbrush down with trembling fingers. 'You'll have to divorce me!'

'Millie, stop it,' he said gently.

'But you will!'

'How long has it been now?'

'Nearly four months!' she wailed, and to her fury he burst out laughing. 'Don't!'

'Come here,' he said tenderly. 'What does that book you've got say?'

Millie sniffed. She hadn't realised he'd noticed her reading it. 'Not to worry until it's been at least a year.'

'Or not to worry at all, more like it,' he said sternly.

'Why aren't *you* worried about it?' Millie questioned.

'What if I told you that I was having too good a time just the way things are?' he said simply.

'*Are* you?' she asked softly, in delight.

'Yes, *cara*. I am. Now, come over here and have a look at the designs for the statue.'

She walked over to him and leaned over his shoulder, looking down at the plans. 'Oh, Gianferro,' she breathed. 'It looks beautiful.'

'Doesn't it?' he agreed, with a smile of satisfaction.

All three brothers had decided that it was high time that their mother should have a monument erected in her honour, and a prestigious Mardivinian sculptor had been given the precious commission. It was to stand just outside the capital, in stunning landscaped gardens with a small lake and tinkling fountain. It would be a place where families could picnic and children could play, and lovers could lie and look at the rare trees and shrubs.

*   *   *

The statue was unveiled six months later, on a beautiful, sunny spring day, and Millie sat with her sisters-in-law—their faces all soppy with pride and love as they watched their three dark husbands bow before the marble image of their mother.

Prince Nicolo. The Daredevil Prince.

Prince Guido. The Playboy Prince.

And King Gianferro. The Mighty.

As the three men walked towards their wives Ella laid a hand on Millie's arm, her face concerned.

'Are you all right, Millie?' she questioned anxiously. 'You look awfully pale today.'

Millie shook her head, and then wished she hadn't as a wave of nausea hit her. 'No, I'm just feeling a bit…under the weather,' she said weakly as a shadow fell over her. She looked up with relief when she saw it was her husband.

'You're not sick, are you?'

Millie met Gianferro's eyes, which were filled with love, as they always were, and some new emotion, too.

Pride.

She raised her eyebrows at him in question.

'No, Ella,' he said softly. 'The Queen is not ill.' Tenderly, he touched his hand to her blonde hair and smiled. 'Shall I tell them, *cara*, or will you?'

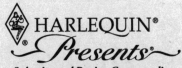

If you enjoyed what you just read,
then we've got an offer you can't resist!

Take 2 bestselling love stories FREE!

Plus get a FREE surprise gift!

Clip this page and mail it to Harlequin Reader Service®

IN U.S.A.
3010 Walden Ave.
P.O. Box 1867
Buffalo, N.Y. 14240-1867

IN CANADA
P.O. Box 609
Fort Erie, Ontario
L2A 5X3

YES! Please send me 2 free Harlequin Presents® novels and my free surprise gift. After receiving them, if I don't wish to receive anymore, I can return the shipping statement marked cancel. If I don't cancel, I will receive 6 brand-new novels every month, before they're available in stores! In the U.S.A., bill me at the bargain price of $3.80 plus 25¢ shipping & handling per book and applicable sales tax, if any*. In Canada, bill me at the bargain price of $4.47 plus 25¢ shipping & handling per book and applicable taxes**. That's the complete price and a savings of at least 10% off the cover prices—what a great deal! I understand that accepting the 2 free books and gift places me under no obligation ever to buy any books. I can always return a shipment and cancel at any time. Even if I never buy another book from Harlequin, the 2 free books and gift are mine to keep forever.

106 HDN DZ7Y
306 HDN DZ7Z

Name _____ (PLEASE PRINT)

Address _____ Apt.# _____

City _____ State/Prov. _____ Zip/Postal Code _____

Not valid to current Harlequin Presents® subscribers.

Want to try two free books from another series?
Call 1-800-873-8635 or visit www.morefreebooks.com.

* Terms and prices subject to change without notice. Sales tax applicable in N.Y.
** Canadian residents will be charged applicable provincial taxes and GST.
  All orders subject to approval. Offer limited to one per household.
  ® are registered trademarks owned and used by the trademark owner and or its licensee.

PRES04R   ©2004 Harlequin Enterprises Limited

Coming Next Month

HARLEQUIN *Presents*

THE BEST HAS JUST GOTTEN BETTER!

#2481 BEDDING HIS VIRGIN MISTRESS Penny Jordan
Handsome billionaire Ricardo Salvatore is just as good at spending
millions as he is at making them, and it's all for party planner
Carly Carlisle. Rumor has it that the shy, and allegedly virginal,
Carly is his mistress. But the critics say that Carly is just another
woman after his cash....

#2482 IN THE RICH MAN'S WORLD Carol Marinelli
Budding reporter Amelia Jacobs has got an interview with billionaire
Vaughan Mason. But Vaughan's not impressed by Amelia. He demands
she spend a week with him, watching the master at work—the man
whose ruthless tactics in the boardroom extend to the bedroom....

#2483 BOUGHT: ONE BRIDE Miranda Lee
Richard Crawford is rich, successful and thinking of his next
acquisition—he wants a wife, but he doesn't want to fall in love.
Holly Greenaway is the perfect candidate—a sweet, pretty florist
with her livelihood in peril. Surely Richard can buy and possess
her without letting his emotions get involved?

#2484 BLACKMAILED INTO MARRIAGE Lucy Monroe
Lia had rejected her aristocratic family, but now she needs their help.
Their response is to sell her to the highest bidder, Damian Marquez,
who wants Lia to provide him with an heir! As the wedding night
looms, Lia knows the truth will out—she can't be his in the marriage
bed....

#2485 THE SHEIKH'S CAPTIVE BRIDE Susan Stephens
After one passionate night, Lucy is the mother of Sheikh Kahlil's son,
and if he is to inherit the kingdom of Abadan she must marry Kahlil!
Lucy is both appalled by the idea of marrying the arrogant sheikh and
overwhelmed by the attraction between them.

#2486 THE ITALIAN BOSS'S SECRET CHILD Trish Morey
At a masked ball, Damien DeLuca is swept away by a veiled beauty
and the evening culminates in an explosive encounter. Philly Summers
recognized her gorgeous Italian boss instantly—he's been invading
her dreams for weeks. But she will keep her own identity secret!

HPCNM0705